SHANNON MCKENNA

CORNER OFFICE SECRETS

Recycling programs for this product may not exist in your area.

ISBN-13: 978-1-335-23299-1

Corner Office Secrets

This edition published by arrangement with Harlequin Books S.A.

For questions and comments about the quality of this book, please contact us at CustomerService@Harlequin.com.

Harlequin Enterprises ULC
22 Adelaide St. West, 40th Floor
Toronto, Ontario M5H 4E3, Canada
www.Harlequin.com

Printed in U.S.A.

Shannon McKenna is the *New York Times* and *USA TODAY* bestselling author of over twenty-five romance novels. She ranges from romantic suspense to contemporary romance to paranormal, but in all of them, she specializes in tough, sexy alpha male heroes, heroines with the brains and guts to match them, blazing sensuality, and of course, the redemptive power of true love. There's nothing she loves more than abandoning herself to the magic of a pulse-pounding story. Being able to write her own romantic stories is a dream come true.

She loves to hear from her readers. Contact her at her website, shannonmckenna.com, for a full list of her novels. Find her on Facebook at Facebook.com/authorshannonmckenna to keep up with her news. Or join her newsletter at shannonmckenna.com/connect.php and look for the juicy free book you'll get as a welcome gift! She hopes to see you there!

Books by Shannon McKenna

Men of Maddox Hill

His Perfect Fake Engagement
Corner Office Secrets

Visit her Author Profile page at Harlequin.com, or shannonmckenna.com, for more titles.

You can also find Shannon McKenna on Facebook, along with other Harlequin Desire authors, at Facebook.com/harlequindesireauthors!

One

Vann Acosta stared at the screen, his jaw aching. "Play it again," he said.

Zack Austin, Maddox Hill Architecture's chief security officer, let out a sigh. "We've seen it ten times, Vann. There's not much to unpack in the video itself. Just Sophie Valente, taking pictures of a computer screen. Let's move on to the next step."

"It's not time for that yet," Vann said. "Play it again."

"As many times as you need." Tim Bryce, Maddox Hill's chief technology operator, put his hand on the mouse. "But nothing's going to change. So there's hardly any point."

Vann gave Bryce a cold look. He was not going to let himself be rushed. As chief financial officer of Maddox Hill, he owed it to his employees to get all the facts, and to study them for as long as it took to get clarity.

"I'll make that call," he said.

"Where the hell did you put that camera?" Zack asked. "It looks like it was recorded from directly behind your desk."

"It was." Bryce looked pleased with himself. "The camera is in a picture frame above the desk. I bought it from a spy gadget website. It has photos of my sons in it. Looks perfectly innocent, but it got the job done."

"Don't get ahead of yourself," Vann said. "Sophie Valente's been personally developing our own data loss protection software. She's teaching our IT department to prevent exactly this kind of data leak, right? It's her specialty." He looked at Zack. "Wasn't that the point of hiring her in the first place?"

"Yes, it was," Zack admitted. "And yes, it seems strange."

"Very strange," Vann said. "If she wanted to steal Maddox Hill project specs, she wouldn't fish for them on Tim's desktop computer where she could be seen by anyone. She's smarter than that. It's far more likely she was conducting a random spot test."

Bryce's eyebrows climbed. "On my computer, at twelve thirty on a Friday night? I doubt it. I made a point of talking about the Takata Complex project in front of her last week, and letting her see the documents on my screen. She knew those files weren't watermarked yet. Drew and his team are still fine-tuning them. I just wanted to see if she'd bite, and she did. The files were copies of old, outdated specs, so she got zip. But I nabbed her. Maybe she can wipe herself off our log files, but she can't wipe herself off my video camera."

The smugness in Bryce's voice bothered Vann. This

was not a kid's schoolyard game. There were no winners here, only losers. "Play it again," he repeated.

"Be my guest." Bryce set the clip to Play. It was time- and date-stamped 12:33 a.m. from four days before. For twenty seconds all they saw was a dimly lit office.

Then Sophie Valente, Maddox Hill's new director of information security, appeared in the camera's view frame. The light from the monitor brightened, illuminating her face as she typed into the keyboard. The camera was recording her from behind the screen and slightly to one side. She wore a high-necked white blouse with a row of little buttons on the side of her neck. Vann had memorized every detail of that shirt. The silk fabric was tucked loosely into her dress pants, lapping over the wide leather belt she wore with it. Her hair was wound into its usual thick braid, hanging over her shoulder.

She lifted a cell phone and began taking pictures of the screen. Her hand moved quickly and smoothly between keyboard and phone as if she'd done it many times before.

But her face looked so focused and serene. That was not the nervous look of a person doing something shady after midnight. She was not shifty-eyed, or looking over her shoulder, or jumping at shadows.

On the contrary. Sophie Valente was in a state of total, blissful concentration.

"Who logged into your computer at that time?" Vann asked.

"Me," Bryce said. "But I wasn't here. I was home watching TV with my wife and son."

Vann stared at the screen. "It doesn't make sense," he said again.

"Facts don't lie." Bryce's voice had a lecturing tone. "I don't say this with a light heart, but Valente is responsible for our data breaches. She knew the documents weren't watermarked. She's avoiding a log trail by taking photos of the screen. What's not to understand? If you're confused, we can go over my data—"

"I understood it the first time around." Vann tried to control his tone, but the look on Maddox Hill's CTO's face set his teeth on edge.

Bryce did not look as sorry as he professed to be. In fact, he looked gleeful.

Still. The man had been at the architecture firm for over twenty years, working his way up the ranks. More than twice as long as Vann had worked there. He'd never been Vann's favorite person, but his opinions had weight.

"What is it that doesn't convince you?" Bryce sounded exasperated.

"Every piece of evidence could be coincidental," Vann said. "We all use multiple computers. She's often here at night. She's responsible for information security. She was thoroughly vetted by the HR department before the hire, and she checked out. We already gave her the keys to the kingdom. Hell, we hired her to code the keys to the kingdom for us. She should be allowed to explain what she was doing before you accuse her."

"Yes, but she—"

"Corporate espionage is a serious charge. We cannot be wrong about this. I won't trash a woman's professional reputation unless we're one hundred percent sure."

"But I am sure!" Bryce insisted. "The data breaches started a month after Valente was hired to head up Information Security. She's fluent in Mandarin. She went to school in Singapore. She has contacts all over Asia, and at least two of the stolen project specs were tracked to an engineering firm in Shenzhen. On top of it all, she's overqualified for her job here. With her credentials, she could make twice as much if she took a job at a multinational bank or a security firm. She had a specific reason to come here, and I think I've figured out what it is. Have you even looked at her file?"

Vann glanced at Sophie Valente's open personnel file, and looked away just as quickly. Yeah, he'd looked at that file. For longer than he'd ever dare to admit.

It was the photo that got to him. It captured her essence as photos rarely did, and it was just an overexposed, throwaway shot, destined for a personnel file or a lanyard.

Sophie Valente's face was striking. High cheekbones, bold dark eyebrows, a straight, narrow nose. Her mouth was somber, unsmiling, but her lips had a uniquely sensual shape that kept drawing his eye back to them. Her thick chestnut hair was twisted into her trademark braid, with shorter locks swaying around the sharp point of her jaw. Large, intense, deep-set topaz-gold eyes with thick, long black lashes gazed straight at the viewer, daring him not to blink.

Or maybe that was just a trick of the light. The effect of the proud angle of her chin. And the picture didn't even showcase her figure, which was tall, toned. Stacked.

Sophie Valente didn't look like a shifty, dishonest

person. On the contrary, she gave the impression of being a disarmingly honest one.

His instincts had never led him astray before. Then again, he'd never gotten a stupid crush on an employee before. Hormone overload could make him blind and thick.

He would not let himself fall into that hole. Oh, hell, no.

"The evidence you've shown me doesn't constitute proof," Vann said. "Not yet."

Zack crossed his arms over his burly chest and gave him a level look. Zack knew him too well. They'd served together in Iraq, and worked together at Maddox Hill for almost a decade. His friend sensed that Vann's interest in Sophie Valente went beyond the strictly professional, and Zack's level gaze made him want to squirm.

"We need more information," Zack said. "I'll talk to the forensic accounting firm I usually use. Meantime, this matter stays strictly between the three of us."

"Of course," Vann said.

"We don't know much about her, beyond the background checks," Zack went on. "Just that she's smart and doesn't miss much, so investigating without her noticing is going to be a challenge. She doesn't fit the profile of a corporate spy. She's not a disgruntled employee with a score to settle, she's not recently divorced, she doesn't have debts, or a drug habit. She doesn't appear to live beyond her means, and she doesn't have a motive to seek revenge. At least, not that we know of."

"How about old-fashioned greed?" Bryce offered. "Those engineering specs are worth millions to outside firms. We should alert Drew and Malcolm and Hendrick. Now."

"I'll handle that when the time is right," Vann said. "When we're sure."

Bryce made an impatient sound. "The time is now, and we *are* sure. I'm not talking about hauling her off in cuffs in front of everyone, Vann. I'm just talking a discreet warning to the bosses. Who will not thank us for keeping them in the dark."

"Malcolm and Hendrick are both in San Francisco for the meeting with the Zhang Wei Group," Vann said. "I'm joining them tomorrow, and Drew's wedding is afterward, at Paradise Point this weekend. Let it wait, Tim. At least until next week, after the wedding. And leave Drew alone. He's busy and distracted right now."

Massive understatement. Drew Maddox was the firm's CEO, but at the moment, he was so wildly in love with Jenna, his bride-to-be, that he was useless for all practical purposes. It was going to be a genuine relief when the guy took off for his honeymoon and got out of everyone's way for a while. At least until he drifted back down to earth.

But Vann couldn't knock his friend. It was great that Drew had found true love. No man alive deserved happiness more. They'd been friends ever since they met in their marine battalion in Fallujah, Iraq, many years before, where Drew, Zack and Vann had shared a platoon. He loved and trusted Drew Maddox.

Still, the upcoming wedding had changed things. Drew had moved into a new phase in his life when he got engaged to Jenna. Vann still belonged to the old phase. It felt lonely and flat back there.

But hey. People grew. People changed. Whining was for losers.

He had nothing to complain about. He liked his job as chief financial officer of an architecture firm that spanned the globe and employed over three thousand people. He hadn't set out to achieve that title. He just did things intensely if he did them at all. An ex-lover once told him he was so laser-focused it bordered on the freakish.

Too freakish for her evidently. That relationship had fizzled fast.

"So how do you intend to investigate her? Is there some way to get her out of the way?" Bryce demanded. "We'll bleed out if we drag our feet on this."

Vann leafed through her file, thinking fast. "You said she speaks Mandarin?"

"Fluently," Bryce said.

"That's perfect," Vann said. "We just found out that they need a last-minute interpreter for tomorrow's meeting in San Francisco with Zhang Wei. Hsu Li just had a family emergency, and Collette is our usual backup, but she's out on maternity leave. If Sophie speaks Mandarin, I could ask her to fill in for Hsu. That way, we get an interpreter, and she'll be out of the investigators' hair. Sophie will be too busy to notice what's going on up here. You know how Malcolm is. He'll keep her running until she drops."

Zack's eyebrow went up. "And have her listen in on all the private details of Malcolm and Hendrick's negotiations with Zhang Wei? You sure that's a good idea?"

"We're not going to negotiate the nuts-and-bolts details of the specs in San Francisco," Vann said. "That's not in the scope of this meeting. It'll be about money and timing, nothing all that useful to an IP thief. It's not ideal, but I think it's worth it, to get her out of the way for your forensic team to do their work. It also gives me a chance to get a sense of who she is."

"Well, they say to keep your friends close and your enemies closer." Bryce chuckled. "Should be no hardship to keep close to that, I'm guessing, eh? Whatever else you could say about the woman, she sure is easy on the eyes."

Vann ground his teeth at the comment. "I'm not yet assuming that she's my enemy," he said. "None of us should be assuming that."

"Uh, no," Bryce amended quickly. "Of course we shouldn't."

Zack nodded. "Okay, then. That's the plan. Keep her busy. Keep your eyes on her."

Like Vann had any choice. Vann glanced back at the computer screen. Sophie Valente's face was frozen in the video clip, her big, clear golden eyes lit by the bluish squares of the reflected computer screen. She seemed to be looking straight at him. It was uncanny.

Bryce got up and marched out of Vann's office, muttering under his breath, but Zack lingered on, frowning as he studied his friend.

"You're tiptoeing around here," he said. "I agree that it's appropriate to be careful. You don't want to ruin her career. Just make sure you're holding back for the right reasons."

"Meaning what exactly?"

"You tell me," Zack said. "Are you involved with her?"

Vann was stung. "No way! I've barely even spoken to the woman!"

"Good," Zack soothed. "Calm down, okay? I had to ask."

"I am calm," he growled.

His friend didn't need to say a word, but after a few moments of Zack's unwavering X-ray stare, Vann had reached his limit. He got to his feet. "I'll go to her now," he said. "I have to tell her we need her for the meeting down in San Francisco."

"You do that," Zack said. "Just watch yourself. Please."

"I always do," Vann snarled as he marched out the door.

Zack was just being thorough. Careful. That was what made him a good chief security officer. But it pissed Vann off to have his professionalism questioned, even by a friend.

Particularly when he was questioning it himself.

He was careful not to catch anyone's eye as he strode through the halls of Maddox Hill. He needed every neuron buzzing at full capacity to interact with that woman, considering how sweaty and awkward she made him feel.

Sophie Valente stood in her big office near a window that overlooked downtown Seattle. The door was open, and she was talking on the phone. Her voice was low and clear and musical, and she was speaking…what the hell was that? Oh, yeah. Italian.

Vann was competent in Spanish, and Italian was just similar enough to be intensely frustrating to listen to. His father had been second-generation Italian, but food words, body parts and curses were all that he'd picked up from Dad.

Frustrating or not, Italian sounded great coming out of Sophie Valente's mouth.

She sensed his presence and turned, concluding her conversation with a brisk I'll-get-back-to-you-later tone.

She looked hot. Sleek, professional. Her braid was twisted into a thick bun at the nape of her neck today, and slim-cut black pants hugged her long legs and world-class backside. A rust-colored, loosely draped silk shirt was tucked into it. She was already tall, but spike-heeled dress boots made it so that she was just a few inches short of his own six-foot-three frame. Her clothes didn't hide her shape, but they didn't flaunt it, either.

There was no need to flaunt. Her body effortlessly spoke for itself. He had to constantly course-correct the urge to stare.

She laid her phone down. "Mr. Acosta. Can I help you with something?"

"I hope so," he said. "I hear you speak fluent Mandarin. Is that true?"

"Among other things," she said.

"Was that Italian I just heard?"

"Yes. I was talking to the IT department in the Milan office."

Then she just waited. No greasing the conversational wheels with friendly chitchat. That wasn't Sophie Valente's style. She just stood there, calmly waiting for him to cough up whatever the hell he wanted from her.

Most of which was unspeakable. And extremely distracting.

Vann wrenched his mind back to the matter at hand. It took huge effort to keep his gaze from roving down over her body. "I'm going to San Francisco for the negotiations for the Nairobi Towers project," he explained. "Our Mandarin interpreter had a family emergency and we need someone last-minute. I was wondering if you could help us out."

Sophie's straight black brows drew together. "I am fluent in Mandarin, yes. But simultaneous or consecutive interpreting is not my professional specialty. I do know several top-notch specialists in Seattle and the Bay Area, however. It's last-minute, but I could put you in touch. Or call them myself on your behalf."

"I appreciate the offer, but both Malcolm and Hendrick prefer to use in-house interpreters," he told her. "The interpreting doesn't have to be perfect, just serviceable. And it's just Mandarin to English, not English to Mandarin. Zhang Wei will have his own interpreter. His grandson will be with him, too, and the young Zhang Wei speaks fluent English. We'd rather have you do it rather than call someone external."

"If that's their preference, I'm happy to help," she said. "But it will slow down the work we're doing on the watermarking, as well as my plans to implement the new three-step biometric authentication process. I had sessions scheduled all week with the coding team, and the project can't go forward without me. That'll be delayed."

"It's worth it to facilitate Malcolm and Hendrick's meeting with the Zhang Wei Group," Vann told her. "I'll make sure everyone is on board with the new timetable."

She nodded. "Okay. Will we fly down with Malcolm and Hendrick tomorrow?"

"They're already in San Francisco, at Magnolia Plaza," he told her. "Be prepared for an intense couple of days. Hendrick, Malcolm, Drew and I have back-to-back meetings scheduled with Zhang Wei and his people all through Thursday and Friday."

Sophie's mouth curved in a slight smile. "I'm no stranger to hard work or long days."

"Of course not." Vann felt awkward and flustered, his mind wiped blank by that secret smile and what it did to her full lower lip. "My executive assistant, Belinda, has the briefing paper she was going to give to Hsu Li. She'll arrange for a car to pick you up tomorrow morning. Talk to her about the travel details, and I'll see you on the plane."

"Great," she said. "Until tomorrow, then."

He turned and walked away, appalled at himself for feeling so sweaty and rattled. It already felt sleazy to gather information on a colleague without her knowledge.

It would be even worse if he got all hot and bothered while doing it.

But there was no question of getting sexually involved with her. He never got involved with coworkers, much less subordinates. That was begging for disaster.

Vann ran his sex life with the same detachment he used for his professional life. His hookups were organized to never inconvenience him. He never brought his lovers to his own home, and was equally reluctant to go to theirs.

He favored hotels. Neutral ground, where he could make some excuse after he was done and just go, with no drama. And he was careful to sever the connection before his lovers got too attached.

He was a numbers guy. He liked control. He kept his guard up. That made him a good CFO, and it had made him a good soldier, too. He was chill under fire. He'd learned from the best.

Sex was fun, and giving satisfaction to his lovers was a point of honor, but emotionally, it ended right where it started for him. It never went anywhere.

Which worked for him. He was fine right where he was.

He had no playbook for coping with feelings like this. He didn't even recognize himself. Muddled and speechless. Distracted with sexual fantasies and embarrassing urges.

He had to stay sharp and analytical. Vann didn't buy Tim Bryce's accusation. It just didn't fit with his impression of Sophie Valente.

He needed to find out more about her to defend her innocence effectively, but that was going to be a hell of a challenge, if just listening to that woman speak Italian on the phone reduced him into stammering and staring.

Not a great beginning.

Two

Good thing Sophie's chair was right behind her when Vann Acosta walked out. The adrenaline-fueled starch went right out of Sophie's knees the second he cleared the door and she plopped down onto the seat. Breathless.

Going to San Francisco with Vann Acosta? Hoo boy.

Please. It was ridiculous to get all fluttery. This was a business trip. She was just a resource to be exploited. Besides, she was almost thirty, wise in the ways of the world and thoroughly disillusioned about men. They were more trouble than they were worth, and they always had some fatal flaw or other. In her experience, the more attractive the man, the more fatal the flaw.

If that rule applied to Vann, then his fatal flaw had to be one colossal humdinger.

Still, even if he miraculously had no flaws, he was

a C-suite executive at Maddox Hill, which was a flaw itself, for all intents and purposes. She was walking a fine line already, juggling a demanding job with her own secret agenda. The firm's chief financial officer was sexually off-limits. A thousand times over.

But Vann Acosta fascinated her. He was the youngest CFO that Maddox Hill had ever had, and he'd held that title for almost five years now. Company gossip painted him as a numbers god. He could have made far more money than he made at Maddox Hill if he'd gone to work for a hedge fund or opened his own.

If watercooler gossip was to be believed, he stayed out of loyalty to Drew Maddox. They'd been comrades in arms in Iraq, along with Zack Austin, who was in charge of Maddox Hill's security. Both of whom, coincidentally enough, were dreamboat hotties in their own right. The Maddox Hill Heartthrobs, they were called. Every straight woman who worked at Maddox Hill had her favorite of the trio, but from day one, it was Vann Acosta who commanded all of Sophie's attention.

It was late, and she had to scramble to reorganize her week, so she set off, stopping here and there to reschedule meetings and tweak deadlines. In the months that she'd been here, she'd found Maddox Hill a good place to work. She hadn't made close friends yet, since she took her own sweet time with that, but she had lots of pleasant acquaintances.

She leaned into Tim Bryce's office, tapping on the open door. "Hi, Tim."

Surprised, Tim spilled coffee on his hand and cursed, flapping his fingers in the air.

"Oh, no!" she exclaimed. "I'm so sorry. I didn't mean to startle you."

"Not your fault," Tim said tightly. "Just clumsy today."

"I came by to let you know that we have to reschedule the team meetings for tomorrow and Friday," she told him. "I'm going down to San Francisco to fill in for Hsu Li. They need an interpreter for the Zhang Wei negotiations. I'll see you on Monday."

"Tuesday actually. I'll be coming back from the wedding on Monday. I won't be in to work that day." Tim pulled some tissues from a pack on his desk and dabbed at the coffee stain on his sleeve. "I'll have Weston email out a memo and reschedule the team meeting. Tuesday afternoon work for you?"

"Tuesday sounds great. Thanks. Have a great week."

"You, too," he said, rubbing at his sleeve. "We'll miss you. But we all must bow to the will of the masters."

She hesitated. "Tim? Is everything okay? Other than scalding yourself, I mean?"

"Fine," he said emphatically. "Everything's fine."

"I'm glad. Later, then."

Sophie made her way into the open plan area, admiring the walls of glass, the towering ceilings and the lofted walkway that led to the corporate offices above. She liked working in beautiful places. Life was too short to hang out in ugly ones.

Drew Maddox strode by. The Maddox Hill CEO was surrounded by his usual entourage, and all the women in the room tracked his progress hungrily with their eyes. She hardly blamed them. Maddox was gorgeous, as well as rich, famous and talented. He'd designed the building she was standing in, the firm's Seattle headquarters. The striking skyscraper was constructed out of eco-sustainable wood products, and the lattice of red-tinted beams overhead was made of cross-laminated timber, as strong as concrete and steel, but much more beautiful.

Drew Maddox had been the first of the Heartthrob trio to fall, after his highly publicized romance with Jenna Somers. His wedding was this weekend, and scores of female employees were mourning their dashed hopes.

But all was not yet lost. They still had Vann Acosta and Zack Austin to cling to.

Sophie was surprised to be on Acosta's radar at all. She'd been introduced to him, but he'd barely seemed to notice.

Better not to be noticed, she reminded herself. She was keeping a low profile while awaiting her chance to make contact with Malcolm Maddox, the company founder. Malcolm was semiretired, leaving most of the decision-making to his nephew, Drew. He spent most of his time in his luxury home on Vashon Island.

Approaching a reclusive, elderly, world-famous architect who seldom ventured from his island home was easier said than done. And Malcolm Maddox was a grumpy, curmudgeonly old man who, famously, did not suffer fools gladly.

Damn good thing she was nobody's fool.

The assignment this weekend was a perfect opportunity to encounter Malcolm, but it came with a hitch—Vann Acosta looming over her, watching her with his smoldering eyes. Distracting her from her mission while she most needed to keep her wits together.

Laser-sharp focus, please. No forbidden lust allowed.

But damn, it was hard. She was a tall woman, at five-foot-nine, but Vann Acosta made her feel like a little slip of a thing, towering over her at six-foot-three. And those thick shoulders? Mmm. She wanted to sink her fingers into his solid bulk and just squeeze.

She loved his rangy build. All lean, taut muscle and bone, with those huge, big-knuckled hands that looked so capable. Those wide shoulders. Pure, raw physical power vibrated right through his perfectly tailored suit and blazed out of his eyes. It made her nervous, in a restless, ticklish, delicious sort of way. She could get addicted to the feeling.

His face was angular; his nose had a bump on it. He had a strong jaw, and his mouth managed to be both grim and sensual. She loved the dark slashing line of his eyebrows. The glossy texture of his thick dark hair.

She couldn't help but imagine how it would feel to wind her fingers into it…and yank him toward her. *Get over here, you.*

Stop it right now. Not the time or place.

Vann had a huge corner office, and his executive assistant, Belinda Vasquez, guarded it jealously. She was a square-built lady in her late fifties with jet-black hair, and she eyeballed Sophie as she approached, her red mouth puckering in anticipatory disapproval. "Can I help you?"

"I'm Sophie Valente," Sophie said. "I'll be filling in for Hsu Li as translator in San Francisco. Mr. Acosta said to speak to you about the briefing paper and the travel arrangements."

"Ah, yes. He mentioned that. I have that briefing paper for you right here." Belinda reached down into a drawer and pulled out a thick folder with Confidential written across the corner. She pushed it across the desk. "That's for you." She pushed a notepad and pen after it. "And write down your address and cell phone number for me to give to the driver, please. He'll be there to pick you up at 3:45 a.m."

Sophie put the folder under her arm, taken aback. "Wow. That's early."

Belinda smirked. "I know, right? Malcolm and Hendrick like to get an early start. Oh, and clothes. It's regular business wear for the meetings, but there's almost always a reception at the end of the second day, so be sure to bring a nice cocktail dress."

"Will do," Sophie said. "Thanks for the heads-up."

"Ah, there you are!" Belinda's face lit up as she looked at someone over Sophie's shoulder. "I was just squaring away the travel details with Sophie."

"Excellent." Vann's deep, resonant voice sent a ripple of emotion rushing up from someplace deep inside her. She braced herself and turned toward him.

"I was about to tell her to hide some energy bars and Red Bull in her purse," Belinda said. "Collette and Hsu Li tell me horror stories about those interpreting sessions."

Sophie met Vann's eyes with some effort. "Horror stories?"

"Oh, those architects just never stop blabbering." Belinda chuckled, shaking her head. "You'll be at it from morning till night, hon. They'll squeeze you dry like a lemon."

"I can take it," she said. "Let 'em squeeze."

Yikes. That had sounded so terribly suggestive. The nervous silence that followed didn't help. Her face went hot.

Belinda cleared her throat with a prim cough. "Well, good, then. As long as you're psychologically prepared for a grind. That's all from my end. Your hotel room is all set."

"I'll fill you in on any last-minute details on the plane," Vann said.

"Great," Sophie said, backing away. "I'll go get organized. See you at dawn."

She'd never seen his smile before. It was more devastating than she'd imagined. She set off, trying not to bump into walls and hoping that no one was watching.

But she had to stay focused. Her secret agenda was top priority, and now she was closer than ever to accomplishing her mission: to obtain a specimen of Malcolm Maddox's DNA for the genetics lab. Not that she doubted her mother's word, but Mom was gone now, and couldn't provide the proof Sophie needed. She was all alone with this.

She had proof already, by virtue of the DNA sample she'd gotten from Malcolm's niece, Ava, some weeks before. The lab techs had assured her that the results were conclusive, so getting a sample from Malcolm was overkill at this point.

Still, it was overkill she felt she needed. She wanted a sheaf of hard scientific evidence in her hand before she looked Malcolm Maddox in the eye and told him that she was his biological daughter.

Three

Vann felt his tension rise when the attendant showed Sophie Valente to her seat, across the aisle, in the small private plane. He hadn't slept well. He kept dreaming of Sophie, and waking up agitated and sweaty, heart thudding.

He was accustomed to being in control. He managed his staff smoothly, pulling just the right strings to get what he wanted out of people. And all that hard-won managerial skill went up in smoke whenever this woman walked into a room.

Sophie gave him a cool and distant smile. "Good morning."

A curt answering nod was all he could manage. He tried to focus on the financials on his laptop screen but he couldn't concentrate. His senses were overwhelmed.

Not that she was showing off. If anything, she'd

dressed down today. She wore a white silk blouse, a tan pencil skirt and a tailored jacket. Her hair was wound tightly into a sleek updo. Little tasteful swirls of gold rested on her well-shaped earlobes. She wore elegant brown suede pumps on her slender feet.

No stockings. The skin on her calves was bare. Golden, even-toned, fine-grained. It looked like it would be beautifully smooth to the touch.

The ultraprofessional, understated vibe just highlighted her sensual beauty. He could catch an elusive hint of faint, sweet perfume as she took her seat across the aisle. He wanted to lean closer, take a deeper whiff.

He didn't do it. He wasn't a goddamned animal. *Get a grip.*

The plane took off, and when they'd reached cruising altitude, the attendant came out to offer them coffee and tea. Sophie gazed out the window at the dawn-tinted pink clouds as she sipped her coffee, lost in her own thoughts. Serenely ignoring him.

This would be the perfect time to start a conversation and start learning more about her, but Vann was stuck in a strange paralysis. It felt all too similar to adolescent shyness. Ridiculous, for a grown man. After a long, silent interval, the flight attendant came out to offer them some breakfast, which Sophie declined.

That gave him an opening, which he gratefully seized upon.

"Now would be the time to fuel up," he suggested. "When we touch down, we'll hit the ground running. There won't be any opportunity later."

Her smile was wry. "Thanks, but my stomach isn't awake at this hour," she said. "It wouldn't know what to do with food."

"You changed your hair," he blurted, instantly regretting it. Too personal.

"From the braid, you mean?" She brushed back the loose locks that dangled around her jaw, looking self-conscious. "The braid needs to be periodically refreshed during the course of the day, or it gets frowsy. An updo is lower maintenance. If it holds. Fingers crossed."

"It looks great," he said. "So does the braid, of course."

"It's my go-to," she admitted. "I finish my morning kung fu class before work, and it's the quickest style if I need to hustle to get to the office."

"Kung fu?" he asked. "Every morning?"

"Oh, yes. It's my happy place. A kung fu teacher came to my high school once to give us a self-defense workshop, and I fell in love with it. It keeps me chill."

"Agreed," he said.

"You practice it, too?"

"Not specifically. I studied a very mixed bag of martial arts. I leaned from my dad. He was a marine sergeant, and a combat veteran, and he borrowed from every discipline, from boxing to jujitsu. He even saw American football as a martial arts discipline. Good training in learning to run toward pain and conflict, not away. So I did football, too."

She gave him a quick, assessing glance. "I can see why your high school would have wanted you on their football team."

"I guess," he muttered, wishing he hadn't started a line of conversation that focused on his body. He was far too conscious of both hers and his own right now.

"Lucky you, to learn to fight from your own dad," she said.

He grunted. "*Nice* isn't the word I'd choose. My father was a hard man. I got my ass kicked on a regular basis. But I learned."

The piercing look she gave him felt like she was peering inside his head with a high-powered flashlight. God forbid she thought he was asking her to feel sorry for him.

"How about you?" he asked, just to change the subject. "I bet your father was glad you learned kung fu."

Her eyebrow tilted up. "Why would you think that?"

"The world is full of sleazeball predators and ass-grabbing idiots. If I had a daughter, I'd want her trained to sucker punch and crotch-kick at a moment's notice."

She nodded agreement. "Me, too. But my dad was never in the picture."

He winced inside. *Damn.* "I'm sorry."

"It's okay," she said. "My mother, on the other hand, didn't know what to think of the kung fu. It's not that she disapproved. She just wasn't the warrior type. Her idea of heaven was a hot bath, a silk shirt and a glass of cold Prosecco."

"They don't cancel each other out," he said. "A person can have both."

"Who has the time? My life doesn't allow for hot baths. Lightning-fast showers are the order of the day."

"Me, too," he said. "When I was in the service, we only had a couple of minutes in the water. You learn to make them count."

Damn. From bodies to baths and showers, which was even worse. Time for a radical subject pivot. "Have you met Malcolm and Hendrick yet?"

"I've seen them in passing, but I've never been introduced. What are they like?"

Vann chose his words carefully. "Hendrick will never acknowledge your existence except to lean closer with his good ear to hear you better. But if you're female, he won't look you in the eye."

"Which ear is his good ear?"

"The left one. Hendrick is extremely shy around women. Any woman who isn't his wife, that is. He worships his wife, Bev. So don't take it personally."

She nodded. "Understood. How about Malcolm?"

"Malcolm is tougher. He's moody, and quick to criticize. He thinks that you should just toughen up and learn to take it."

"Take what?"

He shrugged. "Whatever needs to be taken. So don't expect to be pampered. In fact, don't even expect common courtesy. You won't get it."

She nodded thoughtfully. "Understood. I don't need to be pampered."

"Then you'll be fine. With Malcolm, you're guilty until proven innocent. He'll just assume that you're an incompetent idiot who is actively trying to waste his time and money. Until you prove to him that you're not."

"Wow," she said. "That's good to know in advance. Thanks for the heads-up."

"That said, I genuinely do respect the guy. He has incredible talent. Vision, drive, energy. We get along."

"So you passed his test evidently," she said.

He shrugged. "I must have."

She got that flashlight-shining-into-the-dark look in her eyes again. "Of course you did," she said. "You spent your childhood training for exactly that, right? Getting your ass kicked. Learning to run toward pain, instead of away. It doesn't scare you."

He couldn't think of a response to that, but fortunately, just then, the attendant came through for their coffee cups and told them to prepare for landing.

He shut down his laptop, appalled at himself. What a mess he'd made of that conversation. The idea had been to gain her trust, get her to open up. And without ever meaning to, he'd revealed more about himself than he had learned about her.

And now he had those images in his head. Sophie, hot and sweaty from her kung fu class, stripping off her practice gear and stepping into the shower. Steaming water spraying down on her perfect skin. Suds sliding over her strong, sexy curves.

The harder he tried not to see it, the more detailed the image became.

Soon he had to cross his leg and lay his suit coat over his lap.

Four

Sophie sat next to Vann in the limo as it crawled through rush-hour traffic, trying to breathe deeply. Now she was all wound up with anxiety. She had no doubts about her ability to do the job, but damn, she hadn't counted on being hazed by a bad-tempered old tycoon while she was doing it.

And in front of Vann, too. He just stirred her up.

She'd worked hard on her professional demeanor. Steely control and calm competence were the vibe she always went for. And Vann Acosta just decimated it.

She was spellbound by his dark eyes that never flinched away. Her own directness and focus didn't intimidate him at all.

It felt as if they were communicating for real. On a deeper level.

Please. Stop. She had a crush on the man. She was

projecting her own feverish fantasies onto him, that was all. Snap out of it already.

She was here to do a spectacular job, earn Malcolm Maddox's good opinion and get a viable DNA sample while she was at it. But the last part might be tough, with Vann Acosta watching her every move. It would be awkward if he saw her slipping Malcolm's salad fork into her purse.

She also had to find the time to monitor the traps she'd set for the IP thief at Maddox Hill. Depending on what kind of intellectual property made the corporate spy rise to the bait, she'd be able to interpolate if it was an inside job, or an outside entity.

She'd discovered the data breach within weeks of starting the job, but she was so new here, with no idea who she could trust. Until she had more definitive data, she'd decided to stay quiet about her investigation. Her best-case scenario was to be able to offer the thief up to Malcolm Maddox on a silver platter, kind of like a hostess gift. To set the tone, before she delivered her bombshell about being his biological daughter.

She wanted to make it crystal clear that she had skills and talents and resources of her own to offer. She was not here to mooch.

Vann was speaking into the phone in a soothing tone. "I know, but the traffic is crazy, and we can't control that. Tell him to calm down…Fine, don't tell him…I know, I know…Yeah, you bet. See you there."

He put his phone in his pocket, looking resigned. "Charles will let us out at the North Tower of Magnolia Plaza and take our bags on to the hotel for us," he said. "We're already late, and Malcolm is having a tantrum."

"Oh, dear," she murmured. "A bad beginning."

"You'll make up for it by being awesome," he told her.

She laughed. "Aw! You sound awfully confident about that."

"I am," he replied.

"How so?" she demanded. "You've never seen me in action."

"I'm a good judge of character," he said. "You're tough and calm, and you don't get rattled. Malcolm likes that. He'll be eating out of your hand by Friday."

"We'll see," she said. "Let's hope."

"This is us," Vann said as the limo pulled up to the curb.

Vann held the car door open for her. He led them through the lobby, and then down a long breezeway across the plaza under an enormous glass dome, all the way to the second tower.

"Is this building one of Maddox Hill's designs?" she asked.

"Yes. It was finished last year. Zhang Wei, the man we're meeting, is the owner." Vann pushed the door open and beckoned her inside, waving at a security guard who waved back with a smile. "They want us to design another property in Nairobi, similar to the Triple Towers in Canberra that we did two years ago. That's what we're negotiating today."

"Yes, all that was in the briefing paper," she said. "I read it last night."

"Malcolm and Hendrick and Drew are upstairs with Zhang Wei's team, waiting for us."

"Drew Maddox is here?" She was surprised. "Isn't he getting married this weekend?"

"Sunday. After this meeting, he heads to Paradise Point, and the party begins."

"I've heard about Paradise Point," Sophie said. "That's the new resort on the coast, right? I hope I get a chance to see it sometime."

"Yes, it's a beautiful property," Vann said. "That's one of Drew's first lead architect projects. He made a big splash with it. Got a lot of attention."

The elevator doors hummed open. A woman with curly gray hair and round gold-rimmed glasses hurried toward them, her eyebrows in an anxious knot. "Thank God!"

"Sylvia, this is Sophie Valente, our interpreter," Vann said. "Sophie, this is Sylvia Gregory, Malcolm's executive assistant."

Sylvia shook Sophie's hand and then grabbed it, pulling Sophie along after her.

"Come on now, both of you!" she said. "He's just beside himself. Hurry!"

"He'll live, Sylvia," Vann said wryly.

"Easy for you to say," Sylvia fussed. "I wish you two had gotten here in time to have some coffee or tea or a pastry from the breakfast buffet, but it's too late now. We just can't keep him waiting any longer. Come on now, pick up the pace, both of you!"

Sophie glanced at her watch. Not even 8:20 yet. The guy was hard-core.

Sylvia pointed at two doors as she hustled them down the corridor. "See those two offices? Take note of the numbers—2406 and 2408. The Zhang Wei Group has made them available to Mr. Maddox and Mr. Hill for the duration. If you're ever called upon to interpret for a private meeting, you'll meet in one of those offices."

Sylvia ushered them into a large conference room

with an elegant, minimalist design and a wall of windows. The hum of conversation and clink of china stopped as they entered. On one side of the table was a group of Chinese men. The man seated in the center was very old. Those ranged around him were younger.

There was staff from the Maddox Hill legal department there, as well, but Sophie focused on the three men in the center. She saw Drew Maddox and Hendrick Hill, Malcolm's cofounder. Tall and bald and bony, he gave them a tight-lipped frown.

Then Malcolm Maddox stood up and turned to them.

She'd seen Malcolm in passing, and she'd seen photographs of him online. But this was the first time she'd seen him up close and in the flesh. She finally got why her mother had fallen so hard all those years ago. He was seamed and grizzled now, but still good-looking, with a shock of white hair and deep-set, intense gray eyes. Bold eyebrows, chiseled cheekbones. He would have been tall, if the arthritis hadn't bent him over, and he was trim and wiry for a man with his health problems.

Her mother had fallen for him so hard she'd never recovered. She'd been on a team of interior designers on a project in New York thirty years ago. A luminously pretty, naive twenty-six-year-old with a mane of blond curls and head full of romantic notions.

Malcolm had been over forty. He'd been lead architect on the Phelps Pavilion. Charismatic, seductive, brilliant, charming. Intense.

They'd had a brief, hot affair, and then he'd left, returning to the West Coast.

When Vicky Valente found that she was pregnant,

she'd gone to look for him. His wife, Helen, had opened the door when Sophie's mom knocked on it. She'd left without ever making contact with Malcolm. Mortified. Heartbroken.

Malcolm glowered at them, clutching his cane with a hand gnarled from arthritis. "So," he growled. "Finally deigned to make an appearance, eh? Mr. Zhang, I believe you met Vann Acosta at our last meeting, correct?"

"Yes, we did meet," Vann said, nodding in Zhang Wei's direction. "I'm sorry to have kept you waiting, sir."

"You should be," Malcolm barked. "I don't have time to waste. Neither do Mr. Zhang and his team."

Sophie set her purse down and promptly situated her chair behind and between Hendrick's and Malcolm's chairs. "Whenever you're ready, sir." Her voice was calm.

Hendrick's eyes slid over her and skittered away, but Malcolm's eyes bored into her with unfriendly intensity for a moment.

The meeting got under way with some formal speechifying about mutual friendship and regard and Mr. Zhang's best wishes for prosperity for all in their shared undertaking, etc., etc. Sophie interpreted whenever Zhang or one of the others paused for breath, in a clear, carrying voice. After a certain point, Malcolm's patience began to fray. She could tell from how he clicked the top of his ballpoint pen, a rapid tappety-tap-tap.

Funny. She did that herself when she was nervous. In fact, she'd stopped using ballpoint pens because of that particular nervous habit. She couldn't seem to stop doing it.

Mr. Zhang's speech finally wound up with a flowery expression of best wishes on behalf of the entire Zhang Wei Group for Drew Maddox's upcoming nuptials, and best wishes for the future and wonderful prospects for the happy young couple.

Drew responded with grace, echoing the older man's formal language as he thanked Zhang Wei for his kindness. Finally that part was over, and they got down to business.

It was fortunate that her mind was occupied so completely with translating while she was just inches away from her biological father. Close enough to smell his aftershave, to compare the shape of his ears and his fingernails with her own. His hands were bent by arthritis, so their original shape was impossible to determine, but he had the same broad, square fingernails that she had. The same high cheekbones. Drew had them, too, as well as Malcolm's coloring.

Her intense focus altered her perception of time. She was surprised when they finally broke for lunch. Sylvia approached her as they exited the conference room. "You do know that you'll be interpreting for Mr. Hill and Mr. Maddox during lunch, as well?" she asked, her eyes daring Sophie to say no.

"Of course," Sophie said. "Whenever I'm needed."

"You'll want to arrive before Malcolm and Hendrick get there. I'll show you where to go. Right this way, please."

Sylvia led her onto the elevator and up to the restaurant on the penthouse floor.

When the rest of the party came into the private

dining room, Sophie took her place behind Malcolm and Hendrick and interpreted their conversation with Zhang Wei as they ate lunch. She must have done it competently enough, because no one complained, but very little of what they said penetrated her conscious mind. Her stomach had woken up, and the *fettucine ai limone* and stuffed lobster smelled freaking divine.

No pampering. Belinda had warned her to stuff her purse with protein bars. Vann had advised her to grab breakfast. But she'd been all a-flutter to meet Malcolm up close. And in a tizzy from gawking at Vann Acosta's ridiculous hotness. It was her own damn fault.

As if there'd been so much as a single free moment to gnaw a protein bar today, anyhow.

Lunch dragged on. Dessert, then coffee and still more talk. Global international trade, geo-politics, pictures of Zhang Wei's twin great-grandsons, which had to be admired and chatted about. Still more coffee.

On the way back to the conference room, Sophie trailed Malcolm and Zhang Wei and interpreted as they walked. Mr. Zhang waxed eloquent about the poetic significance of empty space in architecture.

All she got was a pit stop in the ladies' room where she splashed her hands and face in the sink before the afternoon session began. It was twice as long as the morning one, and more technical. This involved Zhang Wei and his lawyers facing off with Maddox Hill's legal department. They got deep into the weeds and stayed there for hours.

At some point in the afternoon, her voice got thick and cracked. Malcolm whipped his head around to glare at her as she coughed to clear her throat.

Then a shadow fell over her. She heard a popping

sound and turned to find Vann next to her, twisting off the top of a bottle of chilled water. Everyone watched in silence as she took a quick, grateful sip. That was all she dared to take the time for.

The sky was a blaze of pink before they wrapped up the meeting. Dinner plans were announced, this time at the restaurant at the top of the South Tower, on the other end of Magnolia Plaza. Sophie was unsurprised when she walked out to see Sylvia approach her with that now-familiar look on her face.

"Same song and dance for dinner," Sylvia said. "Head over there before Mr. Zhang, Mr. Maddox or Mr. Hill arrive. You don't want them standing around before dinner trying to making small talk with no interpreter to help. Mr. Maddox hates that."

Sophie let out a silent sigh. "Of course."

"Are you familiar with the Magnolia Plaza complex? I'll give you a map if—"

"I know it." It was Vann's deep voice behind her. "I'll make sure she gets there."

Sophie followed Vann into the elevator, too tired to feel self-conscious. Her eyes stung, and her throat was sore. She uncapped the water he'd given her earlier and drank deep. "Wow," she remarked. "Those guys have stamina."

"So do you," Vann said.

Sophie slanted him a wry look as she drained her bottle.

"It's true," he said. "Don't think Malcolm didn't notice."

"Oh, please," she said. "He didn't look at me once the whole day. Except to glare at me for being late this morning. And for coughing. Thanks for the water, by the way."

"That's exactly what I mean," Vann said. "Malcolm doesn't reward perfection. He expects it as his due. He doesn't appear to notice if things go smoothly, but if something doesn't measure up to his high standards, by God you'll hear about it."

"So being ignored by Malcolm Maddox all day is a good sign?"

"Very good," he said. "You're excellent. You never missed a beat. I don't speak Mandarin, so I can't vouch for your language skills, but there was good flow all day long. We got more accomplished than any of us expected. Because of you."

"Hmph." She tucked the bottle back into her purse. "It's kind of you to say so. Is Malcolm always like that?"

"Workaholic, hyperfocused, obsessive? Yes. And he expects the same maniacal focus from everyone who works for him. Which makes for some guaranteed drama."

"I was told he was a hard boss to work for," Sophie said.

"He's infamous," Vann said. "You have to be like him to earn his approval. Drew is, at least before he fell in love. His niece, Ava, is, too, in her own way. So are you."

"Me, like him? An alarming prospect." She said it with a light tone, but Vann's words made her hairs prickle with a shiver of undefinable emotion.

Like him? Maybe they did have some subtle, mysterious genetic similarities. But be that as it may, she couldn't be seduced by the idea of getting to know her birth father. When her mother had learned about her stage IV pancreatic cancer, she'd been so afraid at the thought of Sophie being alone in the world. She'd pressed her daughter very hard for a promise that Sophie would approach Malcolm and his niece and nephew once she was gone.

She'd slipped away so fast. Just a few weeks afterward.

Sophie still remembered Mom's chilly, wasted hand clutching Sophie's fingers. *You have more to give them than you have to gain from them. They'd be lucky to know you. I know I was. My darling girl.*

The memory brought a sharp, tight lump to her throat.

She appreciated Mom's effort. It was a sweet thought. But Malcolm Maddox was famously difficult. Even unlikable, by some accounts. The chance that they would truly connect was small. She couldn't let her own loneliness set her up for almost certain disappointment. She'd just fulfill her promise to Mom, and move on.

Vann was talking again. She forced herself to tune back in. "…are kind of like him," he was saying. "I've seen the hours you put in at work. You stay late every night."

"That's more a function of not having a social life than being dedicated to my job," she said without thinking. "I stay late because why not, if I'm on a roll. There's no one at home competing for my attention."

"So you're unattached?"

Heat rushed into her face "I'm new in town," she said. "I just got to Seattle a few months ago. I'm still finding my feet."

The elevator door rolled open, a welcome distraction from her embarrassment. They walked in silence on the cool breezeway beneath the great dome between the two towers, which was nearly deserted at this hour.

"I'm sorry you didn't get any lunch," he said.

"I'm fine," she assured him. "No pampering, right?"

He grunted under his breath as the glass elevator in the South Tower arrived and the door opened.

They got in, and the elevator zoomed up the side of the building. The top-floor restaurant had walls of floor-to-ceiling glass. The ambience was hushed and elegant, and the aromas from the kitchen made Sophie's mouth water.

The host led them to a large private dining room bathed in the fading rusty glow of sunset. A long candlelit table was set for sixteen.

But there was no seat for her. She asked the waitstaff for another chair to be brought in, and was positioning it behind two chairs near the head of the table when they heard Malcolm's deep voice outside the door. He was arguing with someone. The door opened, and that someone proved to be Drew Maddox, looking frustrated.

"...don't see why you should be so concerned," Malcolm snapped. "She doesn't strike me as a type who needs coddling. And these young skinny females never eat nowadays, anyway. No fat, no carbs, no this, no that. Ridiculous creatures."

He and Drew caught sight of Sophie at the same moment. Malcolm harrumphed, and made his way to the table with his cane, muttering under his breath. Drew cast her an apologetic look as she took her place behind Malcolm.

The rest of the party lost no time in sitting down to eat. Vann's encouraging compliments had bolstered Sophie quite a bit, but it was harder this time to concentrate on the conversation without gazing with longing at the artichoke tarts, the succulent entrecôte, seared to perfection and cut into juicy pink slices with slivers of Grana Padano, the gemlike cherry tomatoes and scattered arugula leaves, the rosemary-thyme oven-roasted potatoes and the deep red Primitivo wine.

The aromas were dizzying.

Of course, it would be too late for her to order from room service once she got to the room. It would be peanuts from the minibar if she was lucky. Cue the violins. She hoped the clink of cutlery and the hum of conversation would cover the grumbling of her stomach. Suck it up, buttercup.

At long last, the men from the Zhang Wei Group made their farewells and took their leave. Now it was just the executives from Maddox Hill, and Sophie.

Malcolm drained his wine, and turned to give Sophie an assessing look. "Make sure this one is on call for all future meetings that require Mandarin," he said, directing his words to Drew and Vann. "I don't want anyone else from here on out."

"Actually, she's our information security director," Vann informed his boss. "She's just filling in for Hsu Li and Collette. She usually directs the team on cyber—"

"She's a better interpreter than Hsu Li or Collette. Much better." Malcolm turned his scowl directly on Sophie. "What other languages do you speak?"

"Ah…fluently enough to interpret professionally, only Italian," she told him. "But I'm not actually specialized in—"

"Then it's settled. Whenever we require Italian or Mandarin, you're up."

"Ah…but I—"

"Get some sleep. Tomorrow's another long day. Not as long as I expected, though. We're ahead of schedule." Malcolm frowned, as if fishing in his mind for something to complain about, and then threw up his hands with a grunt of disgust when he couldn't think of anything. "Well, then. Whatever. Good night."

He hobbled out, cane clicking. Drew hurried after to help him to the elevator.

Sophie felt her body sag. She turned to Vann. "How far away is the hotel?"

"Not far," Vann told her. "We're in it already. The first six floors of this building is the Berenson Suites Hotel. Come with me. I'll show you where your room is located."

"Don't we need to go down to the desk? We never checked in."

"Sylvia took care of it. Your bags have been brought up. You're in room 3006, and I've asked for a hotel employee to meet you at your door with a key card."

She gave him a teasing smile as their elevator plunged downward. "What's this I sense? Is this… dare I say it…pampering?"

"It's been a long day," he replied, grinning back at her. "I'd call it survival."

The doors opened onto the third floor and Vann strolled with her down the hall. They turned the corner, and there was room 3006, with a uniformed young man standing by the door, holding an envelope with a key card to her. "Your luggage is inside, miss."

"Thanks so much." She took the envelope and fished out the card.

"And here's your meal," the man said, gesturing at the rolling cart full of silver-topped dishes. "May I take it inside?"

"Meal?" she said blankly. "Ah…no. You must have mixed me up with someone else. I didn't order a meal."

"No, it's not a mistake," Vann said. "I ordered the food."

"You?" Bewildered, she looked at the cart, and then at him.

"From the look on your face in the restaurant, I assumed that tonight's menu would be agreeable," he said. "So I ordered you the same meal. I hope that's okay."

"Oh, dear. Was it so obvious?"

"Only if you were paying attention," he said.

The fraught silence following his reply made her face heat up. She turned away and inserted her key card in the door, opening it and stepping back to let the hotel attendant wheel the cart inside. "I'm ravenous, yes," she admitted. "A hot meal sounds great. But this definitely qualifies as pampering."

"This is just smart management of human capital," he said. "It's stupid to misuse a vital resource just because you always have in the past. Tradition is not a good enough reason to be rude. It's bad business. But Malcolm doesn't listen to me. Not about this, anyway. So this is my imperfect solution."

"Very kind of you," she said. "I like to be considered a vital resource."

"Malcolm certainly thinks that you are."

The hotel employee said good-night and departed, leaving them standing there in awkward silence.

"Well, then," Vann said. "I'll say good-night. Enjoy your meal." He turned to walk away.

"Wait!"

The word flew out of Sophie's mouth against her better judgment.

Too late now. Vann had already turned around, eyebrows up.

"Would you come in and help me eat it?" she asked. "It's a ridiculous amount of food for just one person."

"I had plenty at dinner," he told her. "You've been fasting all day."

"Just have a glass of wine, then," she said. "There's a whole bottle. It's wasted on me alone."

He hesitated, and turned back. "All right. A quick glass of wine."

She had a frantic moment as he followed her in. What had she just implied? Would he misinterpret it? The room was airy and luxurious, with a king-size bed dominating it, but Vann's presence made the place feel breathlessly small.

"Would you excuse me for a moment?" she asked. "I need to pop into the bathroom."

"Of course," he said. "I'll pour the wine in the meantime."

Once she shut the bathroom door behind her, her breath emerged in an explosive rush. She lunged at the mirror over the sink, gasping at the undereye smudges, the worn-off lipstick, the loose wisps around her face and neck. They had gone well beyond the romantically tousled look, and were now officially a straggly mess.

She still had her purse, which was a damn good

thing, since it had her makeup wipes and some lip gloss and mascara. But, oh, the hair, the hair. She pulled out all the pins and unwound the coil. The effect, after a day of the tight twist, was wild waves every which way. The quickest solution was a tight over-the-shoulder braid, but she had nothing to fasten the end. The ties were packed in her toiletries case, which was zipped up in the luggage outside. She could put her hair back up, but that would take time. Her hands were cold and shaking. And he was waiting for her out there.

Damn. She'd finger-comb it, shake it out and act like that had been the plan all along.

Sophie fixed her face with the wipes and a little fresh mascara. She put the hotel's courtesy toothpaste and toothbrush to good use and brushed her teeth before putting on a final slick of colorless lip gloss. It was the best she could do under these conditions.

Toothpaste and red wine, yikes. It was an unholy combination, but hey.

A girl had to do what a girl had to do.

Five

Vann poured out two glasses of wine and strolled over to stare out the window at the city lights. No big deal, he kept repeating. Just a quick drink with a colleague to unwind after a high-pressure day, and then he was out of here, leaving her to her well-deserved rest. No weirdness, no agenda, other than learning more about her and keeping her too busy to notice the forensic investigation under way back at headquarters. God knows when it came to that, Malcolm was keeping her busy enough without Vann's help.

Her stamina was incredible. She was classy and tough. Elegant, composed, pulled-together. That voice, wow. It was a problem for him. Constant, relentless sexual stimulation every time she spoke. Like he was being stroked by a seductive invisible hand.

It kept his blood continually racing. He needed to shut. That. Down.

Sophie Valente couldn't be Bryce's IP thief. A woman as accomplished as she was wouldn't waste her time and energy stealing the fruits of other people's labors. She had plenty of fruits to offer herself. She had that rare quality he'd seen in only a few people, his friends Zack and Drew among them. Ava, too, Drew's sister, and Jenna, Drew's soon-to-be wife. They knew who they were and what they were meant to do on this earth, and they just got on with it, no bullshit.

People like that didn't cheat and steal. Entirely aside from their morals and principles, it would just never occur to them to do so. It would bore them.

Insecure, jealous, damaged people cheated and stole. That wasn't Sophie Valente.

The bathroom door opened. The light and fan flicked off. He turned to speak, and forgot whatever he had meant to say.

She hadn't changed. It was the same silky white blouse over the tan pencil skirt. But she'd kicked off her heels and let down her hair. Her bare feet were slender and beautiful. High arches. Nails painted gold. That flirtatious glint on her toenails made the sweat break out on his back.

Her hair was a wild mass of waves swirling down over her shoulders. Her lips gleamed. Her skin looked dewy and soft. Fresh. Kissable.

"Excuse me," she said, her voice uncertain. "Sorry to keep you waiting."

"No, no. Take your time. It's been a hell of a day." He picked up her full wineglass and presented it to her.

She took it and sipped. "Mmm, thank you," she said. "It's very nice."

He gestured toward the table. "Waste no time," he urged her.

"Don't mind if I do," she said, taking her seat.

He sat down across from her as she loaded up her plate and forked up her first bite. "Oh, happy me. Are you sure you don't want some? I'll never manage to eat it all."

"Positive," he assured her. "Am I making you self-conscious?"

"Maybe a bit," she said, popping a cherry tomato into her mouth.

"I could just go," he offered. "And leave you to it."

"Oh, stop." She grabbed a dinner roll and tore a piece off. "This steak is delicious."

"Glad you like it. Drew and I both complained to Malcolm about not giving you a lunch break. But he's got this hazing mentality baked into his system. Everyone has to run the gauntlet and get clobbered to prove their worth. Classic Malcolm for you."

"You shouldn't have said anything. I can take whatever he dishes out."

"Yeah," he said. "We noticed."

Her eyes dropped. "I heard that you met Drew when you two were in the military together. Is that true?"

"Marines," he said. "*Semper Fi.* Two tours in Iraq. Fallujah, the Anbar Province."

She nodded. "And you've been with the firm for how long?"

"I've worked here for over eleven years," he replied. "Since I was twenty-three."

"And you're already the CFO? Of a big global company like Maddox Hill, at age thirty-four? That's really something."

"I started on the bottom," he said. "After I mustered out of the marines, I was at loose ends. So Drew suggested that I take a job at his uncle's architecture firm. He knew I was good with computers. I thought, what the hell? It might keep me out of trouble."

Her eyes smiled over her wineglass. "Did it?"

"More or less," he said. "I started out as an assistant general gofer and computer guy in the accounting department, and they busted my ass down there. Then the finance manager, Chuck Morrissey, took an interest in me. Fast-forward a couple of years, and he arranged for Maddox Hill to pay for me to get a degree in accounting and get myself certified. After that I was off and running. I got an MBA a few years later. Chuck encouraged that, too."

"No college after high school, then?"

He shook his head. "Almost. I was offered a football scholarship my senior year, but then my dad died. My grades tanked and I lost the scholarship. I couldn't afford college without it, and nobody was hiring where I lived. Central Washington is mostly rural. Sagebrush, wheat fields. So I joined the marines."

"A self-made man," she said.

He shrugged. "Not entirely. Chuck mentored me. When he got promoted to CFO, he made me his finance manager. Malcolm and Hendrick took chances on me over and over again. And Drew went to bat for me every single time I was up for a promotion. I wouldn't be where I am now if they hadn't helped."

"Their investment in you paid off a hundredfold. Out of curiosity, why the marines?"

He sipped his wine, considering the question. "It was a way to test myself, I guess," he said finally. "And learn some new skills."

"And did you?"

"Oh, yeah. I even thought about making a career out of it. But Fallujah and the Anbar Province changed my mind. Then Drew got wounded, and they sent him home. After that, it was pretty rough. I lost some good friends there."

Sophie sipped her wine and waited for more, but he couldn't keep up this line of conversation. The more painful details of his time in Iraq were too heavy, and the atmosphere between them was already charged.

"You said that your dad was a marine," she said. "A combat veteran. Did you join up because you wanted to understand his demons better? You followed in his footsteps so you could make some sense out of it all, right?"

He stared into her clear, searching eyes, speechless. Almost hypnotized.

"Did you find out what you needed to know?" she prompted. "Was it worth it?"

The question reverberated inside him. He'd never articulated that wordless impulse she had described, but the insight rang so true.

His eyes dropped. He took another sip of wine, stalling. Unable to speak.

Sophie put down her knife and fork. "I'm sorry," she said quietly. "That was invasive and presumptuous. Please forget I said it."

"Not at all," he said. "It just took me a while to process it. The answer is yes. That's probably what I was doing, but I didn't know it at the time. And yes, I think it was worth it."

She looked cautiously relieved. "I'll stop making big pronouncements about things that are none of my damn business."

"Don't stop," he urged her. "Make all the pronouncements you want. That way I don't have to rack my brains for small talk. I prefer the crossbow bolts of truth, straight to the chest."

She laughed as she forked up another chunk of her steak. Licked a drop of meat juice off her fingers. As her full, smiling lips closed around it, his whole body tightened and started to thrum. His face felt hot. His back getting damp with sweat.

He had to look away for a second and breathe.

"Your turn," she offered. "You're authorized to ask me any embarrassing question you like. Within the limits of decency, of course."

The limits of decency were feeling about as tight as his pants right now. Vann crossed his leg to protect his male dignity. "Give me a second to think up a good one," he said. "It's a big opportunity. I have to make it count."

She laughed. "Don't think too hard," she said. "It doesn't have to be a zinger."

"Okay, how about this? You talked about being a self-made man. How about you? Are you a self-made woman? How did you come to be so accomplished?"

She nibbled on a roasted potato. "I certainly had financial help," she said. "My mother's parents were well-to-do, and she earned well in her own right, so no expense was spared in my education. But they just assumed I'd do great things as a matter of course. 'From those to whom much is given, much is expected.' That was the general attitude."

"So you're a pathological high achiever," he said.

She snorted into her wine. "I wouldn't go that far. But I ask a lot of myself, I guess. Just like you."

"Do I get a bonus question?" he asked. "Now I'm warmed up. The questions are starting to come thick and fast."

"Go for it," she said. "Ask away."

"Okay. Going back to fathers, what happened to yours? Did he leave?"

Sophie's smile froze and Vann felt a stab of alarm. He'd taken her at her word, and still he'd overstepped. He studied her whiskey-gold eyes, barely breathing.

"He never knew I existed," she said finally. "I can't blame him for being absent."

"His loss."

"I like to think so," she said.

"So it was just you and your mom?"

Sophie's face softened. "Mom was great. I was lucky to have her. She was a brilliant artist. A bright, wonderful person. She was a textile designer, very much in demand. She worked all over the world, but by the time I finished middle school, she'd pretty much settled in Singapore."

"Is she still there?"

Sophie shook her head. "I lost her last year. Pancreatic cancer."

"Oh. I'm so sorry to hear that."

She nodded. "It happened so fast. It took us both by surprise."

"I lost my mom, too," he said. "When I was in Iraq. She had one of those sneaky heart attacks. The kind that seems like an upset stomach. She went to bed to sleep it off and never woke up."

"So you didn't even get to say goodbye," she said. "Oh, Vann. That's awful."

He nodded. "It was hard to find my place again when I came home. Civilian life seemed strange, and I had no one left to care about. So when Drew suggested coming to work here, I thought, what else have I got to do? At least I'd be close to a good friend."

"And the rest is history," she said.

"I guess so. Anyhow, that's my story. What brought you to Maddox Hill?"

Her eyes slid away. "More or less the same thing as you, I guess," she said. "After Mom died, I was out of reference points. I needed new horizons. Fresh things to look at."

"You lived in Singapore before?"

"Mostly. I studied there. Software design. Then a friend of mine who was a biologist had all her research for her doctorate stolen. I was so indignant for her I started learning about computer security and IP theft, and I eventually ended up specializing in it. I learned Mandarin in Singapore."

"How about the Italian?"

"My mom was Italian," she said. "Italian American, rather. Your people must have been Italian, too, with a name like Acosta. I take it Vann is short for Giovanni?"

"You nailed it," he said. "Calabrese. Third generation."

"My grandparents moved from Florence to New York in the seventies, when Mom was in her early teens. She spoke English with no accent, but we spoke Italian at home with my grandparents. I lived with them for half of my childhood. My mom would jet off to do her design jobs, and I'd stay in New York with my *nonno* and *nonna*. My grandfather had a company that shipped marble from Italy. ItalMarble. A lot of the big buildings on the East Coast are made of the stone he imported."

He was startled. "ItalMarble belonged to your grandfather? Really?"

"You know it?" she asked.

"Of course I know it," he said. "We're up on all the providers of high-end building materials. The company changed hands a few years ago, right?"

"Yes, that was when Nonno retired. He died shortly after that."

"I'm sorry to hear that," he said.

She nodded in acknowledgment. "When I was eleven, I persuaded my mom to rescue me. Take me with her the next time she left."

"Rescue you? From your grandparents? Why? Were they hard on you?"

She twirled some feathery arugula fronds up off the plate with her fork. "The opposite actually. They were very sweet to me. But suffocatingly overprotective."

"Yeah? Were they old-fashioned?"

"Very," she said. "But it was mostly because of my health."

He was taken aback. "Your health? Were you not well?"

"I had a heart condition when I was a toddler," she explained. "I almost died a few times. I had to have open-heart surgery. I spent the better part of two years recuperating. After that my grandparents always treated me like I was fragile, and I couldn't stand it."

Vann gazed at the glowing, vital woman across the table from him, tucking away her roasted potatoes with gusto. He couldn't imagine her having ever been ill.

"You don't seem fragile," he said. "Not with the crack-of-dawn kung fu classes, the high-octane male-dominated career and the killer heels."

"I may have overcompensated a little," she admitted. "I push myself. But I never want to feel weak or helpless ever again."

He lifted his wineglass in a toast. "You've succeeded in your goal."

"Have I?" she said. "A person has to climb that mountain from the bottom every single day, forever. You can't just sit back and rest on your past achievements."

"Wow, what a rigorous mindset," he commented. "Don't you get tired?"

"Sometimes," she admitted. "But you know what? It's a lot easier to have a rigorous mindset when you have a big steak dinner inside of you. It was wonderful. Thanks for thinking of me. I can't believe I ate so much."

"Don't mention it. You up for dessert?"

Her whiskey-colored eyes widened. "Dessert?"

"There was a choice of four different desserts. I went with chocolate cheesecake."

"Ooh. I love cheesecake."

Vann retrieved the plate from the tray and placed it in front of her, removing the cover with a flourish. *"Voilà."*

Sophie admired the generous slab, with multiple gooey layers on a chocolate cookie-crumb crust, swirled with drizzles of raspberry syrup. Fruit was artfully arranged next to it: watermelon, pineapple, kiwi, a cluster of shining red jewellike currants, a succulent strawberry and velvety raspberries.

"You have to help me out," she informed him, popping a raspberry into her mouth. "It's too gorgeous to waste, but if I eat it all, I'll hurt myself."

"Try it," he urged. "You go first."

She scooped up the point of the cheesecake slice and lifted it to her lips.

It was agonizing, watching her pink tongue dart out to catch a buttery chocolate crumb. Seeing the pleasure in her heavy-lidded eyes. He fidgeted on his chair.

"Now you." She fished for another spoon and prepared a generous bite for him.

He leaned forward and opened his mouth. That rush of creamy sweetness nudged him right past all his careful walls and limits and rules. He was so turned on it scared him.

He chewed, swallowed. "Wow," he said hoarsely, trying to recall all the bullet points in his lecture-to-self.

Bryce had accused her of spying. Zack was investigating her. She was an employee. A key employee. He was her superior. He never got involved with coworkers. Especially subordinates. Cardinal rule.

He couldn't remember why that was relevant when he wanted this so badly. He stared hungrily as she took another bite of her dessert.

So. Damn. Beautiful.

"Want another bite?" she was saying.

He dragged his eyes away. "I should go. Tomorrow will be another long day."

Sophie's smile faded. "Thanks again. The meal was lovely."

He was supposed to say something polite, something automatic that he shouldn't even have to think about, but the mechanism wasn't working. In any case, he didn't trust his voice. Or any other part of himself. He had to get the hell out of this room.

Before he said or did something he could never take back.

Six

Sophie preceded him to the door, glad to have her back to him for once. She felt so exposed. All that blushing and giggling and babbling. Things she'd never told anyone. And the inappropriate personal questions she'd asked him? What had come over her?

And was he flirting, or just being gracious? She couldn't work it out.

She usually beat down attempts at flirting with a sledgehammer. But she couldn't treat Vann Acosta that way. Nor could she quite tell if it was happening or not.

Ordering her a fabulous meal was a seductive move, but he hadn't tried to capitalize on it. She had invited him in and insisted on sharing the wine. He'd made no sexy comments or innuendos; he'd given her no compliments.

At least, other than for her work ethic and professional focus.

But that conversation had gone beyond flirtation. She had such a strange, electric feeling inside. Like they were connecting on a deeper level.

Soul to soul. The intimacy was jarring. And arousing.

It wound her up. Her toes were shaking, clenched in the carpet fibers. Her chest felt tight; she was afraid to breathe. She was acutely aware of him, and of her own body. Her clothes felt heavy on her sensitized skin. Her thighs were clenched. Her heart thudded heavily.

She reached for the door handle—and Vann's hand came to rest on top of hers.

The shock of connection flashed through her. Her heartbeat roared in her ears. It felt like a sultry fog of heat had surrounded her head.

She was drunk with his nearness. Conscious of every delicious detail of him. His scent, his height. The way his clothes fit on his big, muscular body. The ridiculous breadth of his shoulders, blocking the light from the room behind them.

His eyes locked on hers. A muscle pulsed in his jaw.

She had no more doubt. This wasn't a lighthearted *"How 'bout it, babe?"*

This was raw, stark desire.

She glanced down. His desire was visible to the naked eye. He reached up and wound a lock of her hair around his forefinger, tugging it delicately.

She swayed forward, drawn helplessly by his pull. He was so tall. Her neck ached from staring up at him. Then her head fell into the cradle of his warm hand. His heat surrounded her. The scent of his shirt, his cologne, was intoxicating. Just a little closer and their bodies would touch—and she would be lost to all reason.

His hunger called to her own. She craved it. A big, strong, gorgeous guy who was smart and classy and thoughtful and attentive, a man who wasn't afraid to be real with her, a man who rang all her bells like a church on Easter Sunday. Hell, yeah. Give her some of that. Give her a massive double helping, and keep it coming. She wanted to pull him toward her and wrap herself around him like a scarf. The yearning made her ache.

Then she thought of Mom. Her life blighted by one ill-considered affair with her boss. It was swiftly over, and she was quickly forgotten—by him. But Mom hadn't forgotten.

Sophie saw her mother in her mind's eye, sitting on the terrace of the Singapore apartment with a glass of wine and a cigarette. Every evening, quietly watching the sun set on another day, with that remote, dreamy sadness on her face.

Vicky Valente had never recovered from Malcolm. She'd never bonded with any other man. She'd gone on a few dates, had the occasional brief hookup, but the men always drifted away once she started comparing them to Malcolm.

No one else ever measured up, and she could not settle for less.

That affair had marked her forever.

Sophie sensed the same potential for destruction right now. She was so drawn to Vann. More than she'd ever been to anyone. This could leave a scar just like the one Malcolm had left on her mother. A life-altering wound.

She took a step back, bracing herself against the

wall. "You're my boss." Her voice was unsteady. "This could blow up in our faces."

Vann let go of her hair, and let his hand drop. He started to speak, then stopped himself. "It probably would," he said. "I'm sorry. Good night."

He pulled the door open and left without another word.

Sophie watched as the door swung shut on its own. She felt like yelling in a rebellious rage. Kicking and screaming. What a goddamn waste. Not…freaking… fair.

But the cosmic timing sucked. She was in a state of overload. On the one hand, she was trying to get a DNA sample to verify if Malcolm really was her father. On the other, she was trying to demonstrate to him that she'd be worth having as a daughter.

No one should have to scramble to prove her right to exist. Yet here she was, scrambling for Malcolm's notice and approval and respect. Terrified of not being found worthy. She didn't want to feel that way, but still, she did.

It made her so vulnerable. And that was enough vulnerability for the time being.

She did not need to fish for more.

Seven

Sophie looked as fine today as she had the day before, Vann reflected. She wore closed-toe shoes, but he knew the sexy secret of those gold toenails. She'd left her hair down today, which was a dirty trick. Those heavy locks had slid through his hands like—

Thud. A kick to the side of his foot jolted Vann out of his reverie. He looked around to find Malcolm glaring at him. His boss's gaze flicked to Sophie, who was leaning forward and speaking in a low, clear voice directly into Hendrick's good ear.

Down, boy, Malcolm mouthed.

Nothing slipped past the old man. *Damn.*

Sophie had sensed the interchange, too, and she flashed them a swift, puzzled look while never missing a beat with her interpreting. Thank God they were wrapping it up. They were at the stage of congratulating each other for reaching a mutually satisfactory accord. Zhang Wei had been at it for forty minutes now.

An hour after the meeting concluded they met again for the reception on the observation deck, where the restaurant had laid out a buffet. Sophie was already there when Vann arrived. He stood next to Drew, making conversation with Zhang Wei's grandson while trying not to stare at her. She was dramatically silhouetted against a sky streaked with sunset colors, translating for Hendrick and the elder Zhang Wei. He loved the flounced ivory silk skirt. How it hugged her shape.

Look away from the woman. Damn it.

The atmosphere was finally relaxed. The food and wine were good. After they'd eaten, the younger Zhang Wei was congratulating Drew on his upcoming wedding when Malcolm interrupted, beckoning to both of them imperiously. "Vann! Drew! Come here! I have an idea!"

Vann followed Drew over, careful not to meet Sophie's eyes.

"Mr. Zhang should come to the wedding along with his grandson," Malcolm announced. "They'll both be in the States until the middle of next week, so why not?"

Drew smiled in cheerful resignation. "Great idea, Uncle. The more, the merrier." He gave the elder Mr. Zhang a short bow. "I'd be honored to have you there, sir."

"Damn straight," Malcolm said. "You already have over two hundred and fifty people coming. What are two more? I'll tell Sylvia to arrange a suite. Sophie, too. Mr. Zhang will need to have an interpreter on hand."

He turned on Sophie. "You'll make yourself available this weekend? You can go back to the city on Monday."

"Ah...yes, of course," she said after a startled pause. "I'll let them know back at the office."

"Excellent," Malcolm said. "Vann, you didn't have a plus-one for this weekend's extravaganza, right? I remember Ava complaining about it. Now you have one, so it's a win-win for everyone, eh?"

The younger Zhang murmured in his grandfather's ear. "Grandfather is tired," he told them with a smile. "I will escort him to his room." He turned to Drew. "Will you meet me downstairs at the bar later? I must drink to your last days as an unmarried man."

"With pleasure." Drew turned to Vann. "Join us there?"

"Sure," Vann said.

After the Zhangs made their way out, Sophie spoke up. "Since Mr. Zhang no longer needs me, would you gentlemen excuse me?"

"What for?" Malcolm demanded. "Where are you going?"

Sophie's smile was utterly serene. "The call of nature, sir."

Malcolm harrumphed. "Oh, fine. Off you go."

Malcolm, Drew and the others kept talking after Sophie left, but Vann couldn't follow what they said. His entire attention was on Sophie as she retrieved her purse.

She left the room, and after a decent interval, he excused himself and grabbed his jacket from the chair where he'd left it. He slipped out the door just in time to see Sophie at the end of the corridor, turning the corner.

He followed, peering around the corner when he reached it. She'd gone right past the ladies' room and was approaching the office suite that had been assigned to Malcolm.

She started to look back to see if anyone was watching. Instinctively, Vann jerked back behind the corner.

When he peered around it again, Sophie was gone, and the door to Malcolm's office was closing behind her.

Vann's stomach plummeted into a cold, dark place. He strode after her, wondering if Malcolm had left his laptop in there, unprotected. The old man couldn't quite wrap his mind around the realities of modern corporate security.

Various other Maddox Hill project specs were on it, brought along to illustrate possibilities for the Nairobi Towers project for Zhang Wei and his team. That data could be of great value to an IP thief.

He was almost running. Running toward pain, like Dad had coached him to do in his football days. He pushed open the door of the office, looking wildly around.

The room was dark and empty. Malcolm's laptop sat undisturbed.

Water rushed in the sink in the suite's bathroom. Sophie was in there.

Vann let the door fall shut behind him. He felt almost dizzy with relief. Sophie hadn't opened the computer. She couldn't have, in the little time it took him to sprint down the hall. She might have planned to do so after emerging from the bathroom, but a smart spy would take her opportunities fast. She wouldn't dawdle for one…two…three minutes in a bathroom.

Almost five minutes now. He waited until the water stopped running.

Light blazed out as the bathroom door opened.

Sophie's fingers shook as she tucked the fork she'd seen Malcolm use to eat fruit trifle that afternoon into the plastic bag and shoved it in her purse. It had been hard to interpret Malcolm's and Zhang's conversation while simultaneously following Malcolm's fork with her eyes, memorizing exactly where it ended up on the tray when he was done using it. Hoping desperately that it would still be there, untouched, when she had a chance to get back in here and swipe it. He'd left it laying crosswise over his dessert plate, while the other forks lay scattered around on the tray.

And they were all still that way, thank God. The cleaning staff hadn't taken anything away yet. A stroke of pure luck.

She tucked the plastic bag down into her purse and headed for the bathroom, setting the water running as soon as she locked the door. No toothbrush or razor in here. She'd only find those items in Malcolm's hotel room, and she couldn't risk trying to get in. She simply didn't have the nerve. But she'd seen him take his blood pressure meds and wash the pills down with a glass that he left in the bathroom. That would work.

Two DNA samples ought to do the job. In truth, it was all unnecessary. She'd already tested Ava's DNA from a champagne glass at the company-wide reception celebrating Drew's engagement. The test had demonstrated an overwhelming probability that they were cousins. The geneticist assured her that the test was conclusive.

But even that wasn't strictly necessary. Her mother had no reason to lie to her. Not on her deathbed. She'd always refused to talk about Sophie's parentage. It was one of the few things they had argued about.

Mom had never given in. Not until the very end.

But it wasn't about doubting Mom's word. Sophie needed objective proof for the Maddoxes that she wasn't an opportunistic scammer.

Sophie snapped her purse shut, washed her hands and unlocked the door.

"What are you doing in here?" It was Vann's voice.

Sophie shrieked and jerked back, heart pounding. "Oh, my God! You scared me!"

He just stood by the door, his dark eyes gleaming. The only light in the room came from the bathroom, and the city lights outdoors.

"Why are you here?" he asked again.

"I came in to use the bathroom," she said. "Given a choice between a public bathroom and a private one, I'll always choose the private one."

"This is Malcolm's office," he said.

Sophie felt defensive. "I was in and out of here all afternoon, and I watched people from our team come and go the whole time. I was under the impression that the office was available to all of us. But if it makes you uncomfortable, I'll leave. Excuse me."

She strode past him, chin up.

Vann reached out and gripped her wrist. "Sophie."

It was happening again. The slightest touch of his big hand released that feverish swell of heat, the roar in her ears. That clutch in her chest of wild excitement. "What do you want?" She tried to keep her voice from shaking.

"I didn't mean to offend you. I was surprised, that's all."

"Were you following me?"

He just stood there silently, not admitting it, not denying it. She tugged at her wrist, but he wouldn't let go. "Answer me, Vann."

"Yes, I was following you," he admitted.

"What for?" she demanded.

No part of her could resist as his arm slid around her waist. As his hand came to rest at the small of her back. The heat of it burned through the fabric.

"For this," he said as his lips came down on hers.

Eight

Sophie had spent two nights imagining how it would be to kiss that man. Her imagination hadn't come close to reality.

Her body lit up. A blaze of raw power rushed up from her depths, blindingly intense. His lips coaxed her, drawing her deeper into the seductive spell of his kiss. His fingers twisted into her hair. Her arms wound around her neck. Her heart thudded frantically. She came up from the desperate tenderness of that wild, sensual kiss for a quick, whimpering gasp of air, and then she went right back for more.

The world rocked, shifted. She felt a hard surface under her bottom. He'd lifted her up onto the mahogany desk. One of her shoes dangled off her toe. She kicked it off, then the other one, and wrapped her legs around his. He cupped her bottom, pressing her against the stiff bulge of his erection.

She twined around him, bracing her legs around his as their tongues touched. She loved his taste. The hot, sinuous dance of lips and tongue that promised every possible pleasure, multiplied infinitely. She'd never responded to a man this way. She forgot where she was, who she was, what she was doing, what was at stake. All she felt was him.

The door flew open. The light flicked on. Sophie blinked over Vann's shoulder.

Malcolm Maddox stood in the doorway. He looked horrified.

Damn. Vann felt Sophie go rigid and shrink away.

"What in God's name is going on in here?" Malcolm sounded furious. "Vann? What's the meaning of this?"

Vann pulled away from Sophie's warmth, and turned around to face his boss.

Sophie slid off the desk, shaking her skirt down. She knelt to retrieve her shoes, slid her feet back into them and picked up her purse from the floor, shaking her hair defiantly. "Good night, Vann," she said.

She paused near the doorway, waiting for Malcolm to step aside to let her pass.

"My apologies for the spectacle, Mr. Maddox," she said when he didn't move. "We shouldn't have been in here. But I'd like to go now."

"For damn sure you shouldn't have been in here," Malcolm said. "After two days of watching you work, I expected better judgment from you, Ms. Valente."

Her lips tightened. "Agreed," she said. "Excuse me. I'd like to go."

Malcolm stepped aside to let her pass, then closed the door behind her sharply.

Vann braced himself. This was going to hurt.

"And just what the hell do you have to say for yourself?" Malcolm demanded.

"Nothing," Vann said. "I apologize that it happened here. For the record, I initiated what you saw, not her. She never behaved unprofessionally. That's on me."

Malcolm let out a dubious grunt. "Gallant words, but that looked like equal opportunity bad judgment to me. She should have slapped your face and told you to take a cold shower and grow up. You are her superior. This kind of thing is messy and stupid."

"I understand," Vann said stiffly.

"Only when it's convenient for you," Malcolm snapped. "I never expected you to live like a monk, but think long and hard before you indulge with my key employees. Because it will not play out well for you."

"Yes, sir, I understand," he repeated.

"I doubt it," Malcolm said. "You could hurt her, you know. And when it comes to that, she could hurt you, too. There are very few possible happy endings to a story like this. And all of the unhappy ones reflect badly on my company."

That was true, but Vann didn't want to dwell on it. "I understand," he repeated. "Can I go?"

"That girl," Malcolm said slowly. "She reminds me of someone I knew long ago. Decades ago. Mistakes I made that I still regret."

Vann felt trapped. "Sir, I'm really not sure what that has to do with me."

"I hurt someone back then," Malcolm went on. "I was a selfish dog, thinking of my own enjoyment. I paid the price. I didn't appreciate something special when I found it, and then it was gone. I don't even know why I'm saying this. But I don't want you to make the same…oh, hell. Never mind. Forget I said it."

"If you say so, sir," Vann said.

Malcolm laid his hand on Vann's shoulder. He stared into Vann's eyes with unnerving intensity. "Don't be like me," he said roughly. "Be better than that. You'll thank yourself later."

"Okay," Vann said, bemused. He'd never seen that look in Malcolm's eyes, or ever imagined his boss displaying pain or vulnerability. It was painful to witness. "I will, sir."

Malcolm broke eye contact with a snort. "No, you won't. You'll do as you damn well please. I know it, and you know it."

Vann sidled past him. "Good night, Mr. Maddox."

"Behave yourself," the old man snarled. "Get out of here."

Vann wasted no time in doing so.

Nine

Sophie was surprised at herself. She wasn't in the habit of shedding tears, but getting scolded by Malcolm Maddox when her guard was down—it shook her to her core, and now here she was, blubbering in the shower.

God knows Malcolm was in no position to judge her. But men held women to different standards. Even women they cared about. And she was not in that category.

Nor would she ever be, at this rate. He'd probably written her off already. Decided she was a silly piece of man-crazy fluff who would just wind up embarrassing him.

And that kiss, oh, God. She'd gone molten with desire. She was still dizzy, even after the humiliation of the scene with Malcolm.

What a mess. And she'd thought she was being so

slick, whisking away DNA samples. She'd dropped her purse when Vann kissed her. Ker-plop, down it went on the floor with a glass tumbler inside it. Would have served her right if the glass had shattered.

Sophie toweled off, shook her hair down from its damp topknot and wrapped herself in the terry-cloth robe that the hotel had provided. She brushed her hair and teeth, wondering if she should check on the honey-pots, traps and snares she had laid out for the corporate spy. She'd been too busy and exhausted yesterday to monitor them. She was too tired tonight, too.

She'd nab that thieving son of a bitch eventually, but it looked like her fond fantasy of impressing Malcolm with her smarts and her skills had just gone up in smoke.

In her own defense, it wasn't a fair fight. Vann Acosta was so gorgeous no one could blame her for getting swept away.

The low knock on the door made excitement flash through her like lightning.

Calm down. Could be housekeeping, bringing fresh washcloths and body soap. For God's sake, breathe.

The knock sounded again.

"Who is it?" she asked.

"It's Vann."

The seconds that followed were charged with uncertainty. Images, sensations and memories swirled through her. She felt Vann's big, hot body pressed against hers. His lips, demanding sensual surrender. That vortex of need pulling her down.

If she gave in, it would pull her in so deep and fast she might never get out.

She opened her mouth to ask what he wanted, and

then closed it. There was no point in playing dumb. She either wanted this, with all the risks and potential consequences, or she didn't. She wasn't going to make herself decent. That would be silly.

Vann hadn't come here to see her decent. He came here to get her naked.

She opened the door.

Vann just looked at her. She was acutely conscious of how unprepared she was for this moment. Naked under the robe. Hair damp, flowing loose and wild over the bathrobe. Flushed from the shower. Her face bare of makeup.

No need to state his purpose. She'd stated her own by opening the door. Sophie stepped backward without a word, making room for him to enter.

Vann walked in and turned to face her. "I'm sorry about what happened."

"It wasn't completely your fault," she said. "I didn't exactly shove you away."

"That's why I'm here," he said. "To see if you want this. Because I do. If I read you wrong, or if you've changed your mind, just tell me."

She couldn't speak. Words just wouldn't form in her throat.

"Say something," he insisted. "Please. Tell me where we are with this."

She licked her lips. "It's...a little soon," she said. "Hookups with virtual strangers…it's not my style. I barely know you."

Vann let out a jerky sigh. "I understand." He turned to the door. "I'll go."

"Don't!" she blurted.

He turned back. They gazed at each other in the yawning silence.

There were so many ways to start this. Her breath came quick and shallow, and the air between them felt thick. Time slowed down.

Vann drifted closer. He reached out, touching her lower lip with his forefinger. Stroking it. She vibrated like a plucked string as he slid his hand downward, tugging at the tie of her bathrobe. It came loose and the bathrobe fell open, revealing just a shadowed, vertical stripe of her naked body. Her centerline. Throat, chest, belly, mound.

He had made his move, and now he was waiting for her countermove. Now would be the perfect time for her to say something provocative. To grab his tie, yank him closer. To throw off her robe with a flourish. Ta-da. Take that.

His finger trailed downward. Chin, jaw, throat. He stayed in that strip of space between her robe as he traced the rough, puckered surgical scar on her breastbone, then slid his hand inside her robe to press his palm over her frantically beating heart.

She quivered as his caresses began again. The tender stroke of his fingertips felt so aware, so switched on, so deliberate. Every faint touch felt like a kiss.

Over her belly button. Lower. He brushed the trimmed swatch of dark hair on her mound, then lower, stroking sensitive, hidden folds between. Taking his time. Slow, teasing. He leaned over her shoulder, kissing her throat, his breath warm against her neck. His fingers delved into her secret heat. Petting and probing. Driving her nuts.

She gripped his shoulders to brace herself as she

moved against his skillful hand. He coaxed her arousal higher and higher—until the wave crested, and broke.

Pleasure wrenched through her. A torrent of chaotic, beautiful energy. Deep, pulsing throbs, expanding wider and wider, filling her entire consciousness.

Vann's murmur of satisfaction rumbled against her throat.

Sophie felt wide open to the sky. As soft as starlight. She shrugged the robe back and let it fall. No attitude. No bow-down-before-my-celestial-beauty vibe. She just wanted to be seen by him, known by him.

Vann hid his face against her hair. "Sophie," he whispered. "You're perfect."

She leaned against him, shivering with laughter. "Hardly. With my battle scars."

"Your scar is beautiful. It's the reason you're still here. It represents triumph over death. All the effort it took to make yourself whole and strong."

Her throat tightened. "That's a poetic spin on a big old surgical scar. Nicely done."

"I swear, I could not blow smoke at you if I wanted to. You're taking me apart."

"Me? You're the guy with the magic hands." She looked him over, eyes lingering on the bulge in his pants. "What other secrets have you got hidden away in that bespoke suit of yours? I showed you mine. Now show me yours."

His big grin carved sexy grooves in his lean cheeks as he shrugged out of his suit jacket. He jerked the tie loose, kicked off the shoes, tugged the shirt out of his pants, while Sophie attacked his belt buckle.

He pulled a strip of condoms out of his pocket, and tossed them onto the bed, and then flung his clothing onto the chair. Pants, briefs and socks, whipped off in a few quick gestures.

His naked body exceeded her expectations. She'd seen how tall and broad and solid he was, and she'd felt the intense physical energy he generated. But she hadn't dreamed of the effect his nakedness would have on her. His body was thick-muscled, sinewy and taut and defined. Dark hair arrowed down to his groin. He was beautiful there, too. Stiff, substantial and ready for action. She seized his penis, enjoying the taut firmness, the throbbing pulse, in her palm. The gasp of pleasure he made as she stroked him.

He clamped her hand and held it still. "Stop," he told her, breath hitching. "Let me save it for later. Keep that up and I'll go off like a grenade."

"Sounds exciting," she murmured.

"Oh, it would be, for me. But it's too soon, and I don't want to lead with that."

"No? How do you want to lead?"

His eyes held hers. "Just in case that's a trick question, I don't have to take the lead at all."

"Trick question?" She laughed. "Please. Do I really seem so treacherous?"

"If you'd rather call the shots, just tell me. My master plan is to make you come until you're too exhausted to roll over. The details don't matter to me. Got me?"

She squeezed his stiff, pulsing hardness once again. "Oh, yes. I've got you," she murmured, delighted at the shudder that racked him. "Right in the palm of my hand. It all sounds great. I don't have any sort of master plan, so I'll just enjoy yours. Carry on."

His grin flashed again, and he turned her to face the

mirror, holding her gaze as his hand slid up to cup her breast. Stroking the undercurve. Teasing her nipple.

She sagged back against him with a whimpering gasp. The tip of her breast was a glowing point of concentrated pleasure, and every slow caress racked her with fresh shivers of need. Her thighs clenched as his hand crept lower. His lips were hot against her neck, giving her lazy, seductive kisses that slowed down time. She felt suspended, breathless, as he gripped her hips, caressing her bottom.

She struck a provocative pose, leaning over. "Do you want to do it from behind?"

"Of course," he said. "But not the first time, or maybe even the second time. It's too soon to mess around and be playful. The first time should be… worshipful."

"Oh. So that's what this is? Wow. Being worshipped works for me."

"That's good, because that's what's happening." He pulled the bed covers down and pushed her until she sprawled on her back in the bed. Scooping her hair up, he arrayed it on the pillow, burying his face in it with a wordless groan.

Then he slid down over her body, trailing kisses to the scar on her chest.

She vibrated with emotion as he lingered there, kissing right over her frantically beating heart. Any place he touched began to glow and melt into something shining and liquid. His touch was magic. Transforming her.

After a sweet, languorous eternity of kisses, he trailed them down over her breasts, then her belly. Farther, and then farther down, kissing and licking and nuzzling, until he settled between her thighs and put his mouth to her most sensitive flesh.

And she could do nothing but shiver and gasp.

Ten

Worshipful.

It wasn't a tactic, or a choice. It was a stark truth, a physical necessity, like breathing. His body worshiped hers. Some part inside him bowed before her, dazzled by her beauty. Humbled by the privilege of touching her, pleasing her. Tasting her.

She was so sweet. He'd never imagined anything as exciting as caressing her secret female flesh with his tongue, taking his time. Making it last. Making her wait. The longer he made this last, the bigger the payoff.

Finally, she exploded in another shattering orgasm. He savored it, and kissed his way back up her body, settling himself over her. "You're good?" he asked.

Sophie smiled as her eyes fluttered open. "You couldn't tell?"

"I take nothing for granted with you," he said. "It's too important."

"It's wonderful," she whispered. "It's superdeluxe. Please, proceed with your master plan. As a matter of fact..." She grabbed the pack of condoms that he'd tossed on the bed and opened one. She put the little circle of latex in his hand, and slid her fingers into his chest hair, gripping until he felt the bite of her nails. "Don't make me wait."

Vann was teetering on a tightrope of self-control. He got the condom on with no fumbling. Then she pulled him into her arms, wiggling until she had him right where she wanted him...slowly easing deeper into her tight, clinging heat.

Then the deliberate, rocking surges, jaw clenched, panting for control as he fought the urge to go crazy. Lose control.

No. He was sticking to the plan. Oh-so-slow. Until it was too slow for Sophie, and she was winding her legs around his and insisting with her body. Her nails dug into him. She made those whimpering sounds that made him want to explode...but he hung back. Just a little longer...until her felt her climax start to overtake her.

Then he was lost. The power crashed through him, obliterating thought.

Afterward, he felt her lips against his cheekbone. Her chest jerked and heaved.

Still inside her, he rolled off to let her breathe. He was amazed by her beauty. He could hardly believe she was real. He drew away with extreme reluctance. "I have to get rid of the condom," he said. "Don't go anywhere. Please."

"Don't worry," she murmured. "I can't move."

He slid off the bed and went into the bathroom to take care of it, then slid right back into bed with her, tugging the sheet up over the two of them. Hungry for contact. She was so long and lithe and exquisitely smooth. Her soft curves. Those high, full breasts.

She snuggled up close, and her pink tongue licked his collarbone, making his body instantly stir. "You taste good," she whispered. "So salty."

"You, too," he told her. "You're so sweet. Can't get enough of you."

Her full lips curved in that seductive smile. "Awww." Sophie slid her fingers through his sweat-dampened hair, exploring him. Neck, shoulder. Squeezing and murmuring her approval. "This is going to get us into so much trouble."

"Is it?" he said.

"You saw how Malcolm reacted. He's angry. And disgusted."

"He has the wrong idea about us."

"How so?"

He pulled her closer, wrapping his leg around her body. "He thinks I'm just serving myself. Using you. That's not what's happening here."

She laughed. "If you are using me, then you're doing a damn good job of it."

"All jokes aside, it was never about that," he told her. "This is like nothing I've ever felt before."

"I'm glad. Because honestly? I do not feel used right now."

"What do you feel?" He blurted out the question without considering whether he was ready to hear the answer.

She considered the question for a moment. "Hmm, let me think," she said. "Sexually satisfied. Flattered. Delighted. Infinitely pleasured. And definitely pampered."

"That's a good starting place," he said, relieved.

"Also worried," she added. "About the fallout."

"We'll get through it," he said. "We'll look back on this and laugh."

She gave him a dubious look. "I'm not sure what that means. But it sounds hopeful."

"It is hopeful," he said forcefully. "As a matter of fact, I haven't felt this hopeful in…well, hell. I don't know. Ever, maybe."

Her eyes widened. "Vann. Put the brakes on. We hardly know each other."

"We can fix that," he suggested. "This weekend is the perfect opportunity. We'll accelerate the process. We can work at it every waking moment. I want to learn all your secrets. I want to know everything about you. Hopes, dreams, fears, nightmares."

To his dismay, Sophie pulled away. She sat up, tossing her hair back over her shoulder. "Okay," she said, her voice guarded. "But let's take it easy."

"Easy how?" he demanded. "What does that even mean?"

"I'm not an invited guest, Vann," she reminded him. "I'm hired help, remember? I'm a convenience for Zhang Wei. I'll be at his beck and call, not yours. You won't have a chance to learn my secrets while I'm following Zhang around. And Malcolm will definitely be watching us like a hawk after tonight."

"I don't care." He realized, as the words came out, that they were literally true.

"Well, I still do," she said. "So don't rush me."

Sophie slid off the bed, giving him the opportunity for a long, appreciative look at her backside, that mass of dark hair swinging against her back, the perfect curves of her bottom. The pearl-like luster of her skin. Those long, shapely legs.

She uncorked the wine he'd ordered the night before, and took the paper caps off the two water tumblers that were on the tray, pouring out two glasses. Then she sauntered back, aware of his gaze. Taking her time. Letting him look.

She handed him a glass. "One step at a time," she said. "Let's not get ahead of ourselves."

"Why not?" he demanded, rebellious.

"It's not smart to push our luck."

He shrugged. "I have never felt so lucky in my life."

She sipped her wine as she studied him, gorgeous and enigmatic in the darkness. He suddenly thought of Tim Bryce and his accusations.

They seemed even more ridiculous now. He'd met liars and cheats. Some were attractive, smart, charming, but none of them shone like Sophie. Strength and toughness radiated out of her, impossible to mistake.

Sophie was for real. He'd bet everything he had on that.

"It doesn't scare you?" she asked him. "Feeling so lucky?"

He shrugged. "Sure, it scares me. So what? I'll be brave."

She came closer, placing her glass on the bedside table, and clambered onto the bed, flinging her leg over his thighs. "Okay," she said softly. "Let's be brave. Careful…but brave." She kissed his chest, her gaze flicking up at him with a teasing smile as her kisses trailed lower.

"Whoa," Vann said. "What are you doing?"

"Getting to know you," she said. "Didn't you say you wanted to accelerate the process?"

"Of course. But…ah… I thought you wanted to slow down."

She pressed a kiss to his thigh, her hand caressing his shaft. "But then we decided to be brave, right?"

"Uh…yeah," Vann choked out as she took him in her mouth.

And that was the end of any words.

Sophie floated in bliss. Her body was lapped by it, caressed and cradled and rocked by waves of pleasure as she drifted up, closer to waking consciousness—

Just in time for the explosive burst of release. It welled up from some mysterious source inside her, radiating out into the universe like the sunrise.

Her eyes fluttered open as pleasure echoed through her. She looked down, gasping for breath. Vann lay between her legs, kissing the side of her thigh, petting her tenderly with his fingertips. Smiling at her as he wiped his mouth.

"Couldn't resist," he said. "Thought it might be a good way to start the day."

Wow. She could not voice the word. She just formed it with her lips.

Vann rose up, a condom ready in his hand. "Am I overdoing it?"

She shook her head and held out her arms, and Vann rolled the latex swiftly over his impressive erection. He covered her with his warmth, resting on his elbows.

Her body's response was instinctive, immediate. She arched and opened as he pressed slowly inside her.

Their breath was ragged, eyes locked with each slow, surging thrust. Each stroke a caress, a sweet lick of pure delight.

It was harder to look into his eyes in the light of dawn, with the day ahead of them, with all its dangers and uncertainties. The night they'd passed was a wild erotic dream of sensual delights. She'd been so wanton, surrendering to pleasure, over and over again.

He'd awakened a need that got bigger, hotter and wilder every time.

They moved frantically against each other, desperate for release…and came to pieces together.

Vann rolled to the side, breathing raggedly. They lay there, stroking each other's damp skin. Speechless with emotion. He seized her hand, and kissed it.

"You remember that we have a plane to catch this morning, right?" she asked.

He nodded, still kissing her knuckles. "There's still time."

"There's always less than you think," she said. "And remember. Be discreet."

"If you want."

"You don't want? You want to throw caution to the wind? Already?"

He shrugged. "I'm not ashamed," he said.

"Well, I'm not ashamed, either. But for now, I don't want anyone else to know about what's between us. It's new and fresh. Let's protect it from the outside world for a while."

"That's fair."

She laughed at him. "And to that end, you should get

back to your room before anybody sees you wandering the halls with bedhead and lipstick stains."

"Do I have lipstick stains?" His eyes widened. "Cool. Where?"

She swung a pillow at him, laughing. "Oh, get out."

"I'm dismissed? Already?" he asked, crestfallen.

"Just for now," she said demurely. "Later, we'll see. Don't you need to pack?"

Vann headed into the bathroom with a long-suffering look. He emerged a few minutes later, hair damp, and pulled on his clothes. "See you downstairs."

"Downstairs," she echoed.

The door shut behind him, and the room felt unbearably empty and quiet.

Sophie rolled over, pressing her face against the pillow to bury a scream of pure emotional overload. Excitement, terror, shock, joy.

And hope. This had been beyond anything she'd ever imagined. She was head over heels in lust. She'd fallen into bed with a guy she hardly knew. She'd given him everything she had to give.

And now all she could do was count the hours until she could do it again.

Eleven

Sophie was good at playing it cool. She greeted Vann at the coffee bar in the hotel restaurant with the same crisp friendliness with which she greeted Drew and the others. No one would have known they had passed a night of searing passion.

Except Drew, who knew him well. As soon as Sophie went to the buffet for some scrambled eggs and fruit, he spoke up.

"Zhang and I missed you last night at the bar," he said. "I thought you said you'd meet us. We waited for you for quite some time."

"Oh. Ah, yeah." Vann had completely forgotten. "Sorry. I ended up getting involved in some work stuff in my room."

"Yeah? I texted you. Several times." Drew's voice was carefully nonchalant.

"Sorry I missed it."

"Came by your room, too, on my way to bed. Knocked on your door. Pretty loudly. Guess you must have crashed hard. Long day yesterday, hmm?"

"I was wearing headphones," Vann said through his teeth. "I blast heavy metal when I'm looking at numbers. It keeps me focused."

"Oh. I see." Drew's eyes flicked over to Sophie, and then back to Vann. "Well, good luck with those numbers. I hope they all add up for you."

Vann's phone chimed. When he got it out he saw the four messages from Drew from the night before. And one from Bryce that had just arrived.

Learn anything about SV?

Tension gripped him. It offended him that Bryce was so convinced that Sophie was the spy. As if Bryce had accused Vann himself.

Nothing, he texted back. Not her. One hundred percent sure of that.

He could feel Bryce's irritation in the quickness of the man's response.

Didn't try too hard, did you?

Vann texted back rapidly. Malcolm invited her to the wedding to interpret for the Zhangs. Suspend everything. You're barking up the wrong tree. Look elsewhere.

Wrong tree, my ass, Bryce texted back. SV at P Point this weekend is perfect. We'll settle this. I'll call a meeting with Malcolm, Hendrick, Drew and SV when you get to P Point. Do not tip her off.

Don't do this, Vann texted. Not at the wedding. Not the place or time.

Bryce did not respond. *Shit*.

"Vann?"

He looked up at the sound of Sophie's voice, and thumbed the app closed. "Yes?"

"The others are waiting in the car," she said. "Time to go."

"On my way." He slid his phone into his pocket and followed her.

Sylvia was in the lobby, looking harassed as always. "There you are! I had them go ahead and load your luggage. Malcolm is getting agitated!"

Vann suppressed a rude suggestion about what Malcolm could do with his agitation. "Thanks, Sylvia," he said. "I appreciate your help."

"Thank God someone does," Sylvia snapped.

The one free spot in the limo was right next to Sophie. Her sweet scent was dangerously overstimulating. Drew sat in the front, while Hendrick, the Zhangs and Malcolm were in the other car.

"They don't need me to interpret over there?" Sophie asked.

"Zhang's grandson can manage," Drew said. "At the wedding he'll probably do most of the interpreting for his grandfather, anyway. You won't have to work like you did these last couple days. You'll be able to relax and enjoy yourself."

Sophie looked doubtful. "Ah. Well, in that case, should I even go at all?"

"Yes, by all means," Drew urged. "For backup. Just

in case. At this point, my uncle would pitch a fit if you pulled out. You can be Vann's plus-one. He's always throwing off the seating arrangements by refusing to bring a date."

Sophie gave Vann a quick, teasing glance and patted his knee. That tiny brush of contact made his heart race and his face flush.

Bryce could not be allowed to mess with her. He'd never met anyone so clear and honest and real, and he was going to make damn sure all the people who counted knew it.

But it made his guts chill to think how Sophie would feel if she knew that doubts had been cast on her character. She'd feel mortified and betrayed.

If he could shield her from that, he would. If he was careful, she might never even know.

They were picked up at the Sea-Tac Airport by another pair of limos, and they set off straight to Paradise Point. As they drove, Sophie pondered the relative merits of the two cocktail dresses she'd brought, longing for fresh wardrobe options. Neither dress was perfect for the occasion, but that was just too damn bad. She'd probably go with the dusty-pink one with the chiffon wrap.

Her phone beeped, and she checked it. It was a message from Tim Bryce.

Heard you were going to be at Paradise Point. Calling a quick emergency meeting this morning before the rehearsal dinner. See you there. Tim.

She looked at Vann. "No rest for the wicked, I'm

afraid. Tim called a meeting. Five o'clock. What could possibly be so urgent, I wonder."

"Count me out," Drew said. "I've been waiting to see Jenna for days. The minute I get to Paradise Point, I'm officially unavailable until after the honeymoon."

"Right," Vann said. "The rest of us grunts can pick up the slack."

"Don't even try to guilt me." Drew grinned widely over his shoulder. "Wasted effort. I'm too buzzed to notice or care."

The car had turned onto a long driveway through a blaze of spectacular spring wildflowers. Evening sunshine slanted through them, lighting up the blossoms like stained glass, glinting around the edges of the clouds over the ocean.

The entrance to the Paradise Point Resort was a glassed-in reception hall with a wooden roof made of big interlocking geometric triangles. A wall of glass at the end of the building looked out on a terrace, the grounds and the ocean cliffs.

Malcolm turned to them. "I've been told that Tim Bryce just called a meeting, God knows why. The resort has kindly made the southwest conference room available to us. The rehearsal dinner begins in less than two hours, so let's get this dealt with."

Tim Bryce was waiting in the conference room. He jumped up as they came in.

"Congratulations, sir," he said to Malcolm. "I heard the negotiations went well."

"They were fine," Malcolm snapped. "So what in God's name is so important that it can't wait until next week?"

"Ah, well, sir, when I learned that Mr. Zhang was

here, it occurred to me that now was the best opportunity to show him the latest eco-engineering that Drew's team developed for the Johannesburg project," Tim said. "There's a lot of overlap. We've been keeping them in the vault until the new security technology is in place, but being able to show them to Mr. Zhang was worth the risk." He indicated the laptop on the table. "So here they are."

"And this couldn't have waited until after the rehearsal dinner?"

"I thought it was better to know right away, so that you could schedule—"

"Thanks, Tim." Malcolm snatched up the laptop. "I'll take this for safekeeping." He looked at Sophie. "Our interpreter will make herself available to discuss these plans with Mr. Zhang whenever we can carve out a free hour."

"Of course, sir," she assured him.

"Excellent. Sylvia has your number. She'll let you know when we need you." He clapped his hands. "So! We're done, correct? Or is there more?"

"That was the main issue, but I also—"

"Good. Then let's get ready for this rehearsal dinner." Malcolm squinted at Sophie. "You come, too. You're Vann's plus-one."

"Me?" she said, alarmed. "Why? Do I need to interpret? Will Mr. Zhang be there?"

"No, he'll be resting," Malcolm said. "Come to the dinner, anyway."

"But I barely know the groom, and I've never even met the bride!"

"You're Vann's plus-one, and I want you there,"

Malcolm said testily. "Don't be late." He stomped out, the laptop clutched under his arm.

Sophie turned to Vann. "This is awkward. A rehearsal dinner is an intimate gathering. It's already strange that I'm at this wedding at all."

"Don't bother arguing," Vann advised. "You'll only hurt yourself. And don't worry about the crowd. They're all nice people, and they understand how Malcolm is. You'll like them."

"I'd better go make myself decent," Sophie said.

"I'll be waiting for you in the front hall at eight thirty," he told her.

She gave him a grateful smile and set off, consulting the map of the grounds the reception staff had given her. She was in number 82, the Fireweed Cabin. Wooden walkways led out from the main reception hall like the branches of a tree out from the trunk, each winding branch leading to a cluster of individualized cabins.

It was a beautiful walk. The wooden pathway led around jagged rock formations, ferns sprouting below the walkway, vines and flowers sprawling over the wooden boards. Flowers were everywhere. Much of the walkway was shaded with huge, fragrant pines and firs, and stunted, wind-twisted madrone trees. The sinking sun outlined the clouds with shining gold, and the sea's constant roar in the distance filled her ear.

She found the Fireweed Cabin, unlocked the door—and jerked back with a gasp.

Someone was already inside.

The woman shrieked, dropping something on the floor. "Oh, God! You scared me half to death!"

Sophie looked at the number written on her card.

"Excuse me, but my card envelope says 82. Am I in the wrong room? This is 82, right? Fireweed Cabin?"

"Yes, it is, and no, you are not in the wrong room." The woman was young and rosy-cheeked with a high, bouncing blond ponytail. "I'm resort staff."

Sophie registered the maroon jacket and black pants, as well as the name tag on the woman's ample chest. "Oh. I see. I'm sorry I startled you."

"Not at all," the woman said. "I gave you a scare, too, I imagine. I was just bringing your bags to your room from the reception hall."

Sophie realized belatedly that the stuff spread over the bed were her own clothes. "Why are my things out on the bed?"

"Oh, I'm so sorry about that." The woman gave her an anxious smile. "Your garment bag slid off the luggage cart and fell into one of the swampy bits. It rained last night, see, and there's some bits that don't drain very well. Your bag got mud on it, so I was just getting your things out and making sure they were okay before water seeped through and stained them. I know it's kind of strange, but I figured, if it was me, I'd prefer having my stuff rescued than finding a wardrobe crisis on my hands."

"I see." The woman's name tag read "Julie," she saw as she came inside. She leaned to touch the garment bag, unzipped on the floor. It was sodden, as Julie had said.

"I took a washrag and sponged off the mud," Julie explained. "I'm so sorry this happened. I hope you don't mind me taking the liberty of trying to save your clothes."

"No, I guess I appreciate the effort," she said. "Did anything get ruined?"

"No, thank God." Julie's toothy smile blazed at full wattage. "Everything seems just fine! Shall I hang your clothes up for you?"

"No, thanks," Sophie said. "I'll take it from here. Have a nice evening."

"You, too!" Julie crouched down and grabbed a smartphone up off the floor, slipping it into her pants pocket. "Sorry. I was so startled I dropped it when you came in."

Sophie watched the woman leave with mixed feelings. She didn't care for having her private things handled by a stranger, but in Julie's position, she might have made the same call, even if it was an invasion of privacy.

Sophie draped the sodden garment bag over the luggage rack to dry and hung her clothes up. She'd thought she was overdoing it when she packed three days ago. Now she wished she'd brought a much wider selection.

She took a quick shower, then let her hair down and shook it loose. The tight twist gave it enough curl and movement so that it looked quasi-styled. She put on the bronze knit top and white flounced silk skirt that she'd worn yesterday. Drew, Malcolm and Vann had already seen it, but if she wanted a fresh dress for the wedding, she had to recycle this one tonight.

After freshening up her makeup, dabbing on perfume and sliding on her heels, she was ready. Malcolm had insisted, so there was no help for it.

Time to crash her long-lost cousin's wedding.

Twelve

Vann lingered by the entrance to the dining room, keeping his eyes trained on the walkway outside. Sophie was already at a disadvantage tonight. He wasn't letting her walk into a room full of strangers all alone.

Tim Bryce strolled in, caught sight of Vann and started toward him.

Hmm. This might get interesting.

The other man stopped at a safe distance. "You're not doing yourself any favors, you know."

"What the hell is that supposed to mean?" Vann asked.

Bryce smiled thinly. "You know exactly what I'm talking about."

Vann's hands had balled into fists. He forced them to relax. "What you're doing is a pointless waste of time and resources. I've already told you it's not her. This is supposed to be a celebration. Do not mess it up."

"I won't ruin Drew's precious wedding," Bryce said. "I'll be discreet. The fallout can wait." He gave Vann a meaningful look. "Unless you tip her off, that is."

Rage made the hair prickle on his neck. "What are you implying?"

Bryce shrugged. "It just seems strange. You've been her biggest champion, from the very start. You really, really don't want it to be her. And anyone with half a brain could figure out why. That makes your judgment suspect."

"She doesn't need a champion," Vann said through his teeth.

"Well, be that as it may. You'd better not say anything to her. Because she's the one, Vann. There's no doubt in my mind. The truth will come out, and when it does, you'll be implicated. And it will not go well for you."

Vann's jaw ached. "Whatever you're plotting, she won't take the bait."

"Shhh." Bryce's gaze fixed over Vann's shoulder, at someone behind him.

"Good evening, gentlemen." It was Sophie's voice, coming up behind him.

Vann turned around. The sight of her was like a punch to the chest. Her gold-kissed skin, her luxurious hair swirling loose, those let-me-fall-into-your-infinitely-deep eyes. She wore the same outfit as yesterday, and he liked it even better tonight. Her smiling lips shone with a shimmery, gold-toned lipstick. She looked like a goddess.

He caught the expression on Bryce's face as the

man looked away. That knowing smirk, like Bryce had something over him. *Bastard.*

"Hey, Tim," Sophie said. "Are you coming to the rehearsal dinner, too?"

"No, not me," Bryce replied. "I'm just out here waiting for my son Richard. He drove up from LA, and should be arriving soon. He and I are having dinner later on."

"Oh. So your son knows Drew?" she asked.

"They went to high school together," Bryce told her. "Now Richard works on CGI for a movie studio down in Hollywood."

"That's wonderful," Sophie said. "I look forward to meeting him tomorrow."

Bryce turned a meaningful gaze on Vann. "Have a good time at the rehearsal dinner. Remember what I said. Not one word." He nodded at Sophie, and walked away.

Sophie gazed after him, puzzled. "What was that about?"

Vann shook his head. "Nothing," he muttered. "Just some accounting stuff. Shall we go on in?" He offered her his arm.

She took it, smiling. "Thanks for waiting for me."

Vann introduced her to people as they circled the table. Bev, Hendrick's wife. Jenna, the bride. Then Ava, Drew's sister, and Cherise, one of Jenna's bridesmaids.

Sophie was seated between Vann and Cherise. Today Cherise was sporting a bright purple and crimson forelock that dangled playfully between her eyes. She had a mechanical arm decorated with flashing accent lights, and it seemed to do anything she wanted it to do. Cherise had gotten her bionic arm from Jenna's foundation, Arm's Reach. She'd since become one of Jenna's closest friends. Several other people Vann had met from Jenna's foundation were also at the table.

"Nice work, Vann," Cherise said, eyeing Sophie with approval. "She's a hottie. Let me load you guys up with some of this fabulous bubbly." She poured everyone champagne, demonstrating total mastery of her state-of-the-art prosthetic. Sophie couldn't help but be in awe.

His friends toasted Cherise's progress while giving him and Sophie that considering look. Drew must have said something to Jenna about them and God only knew what Jenna had said, and to whom.

Fortunately, Cherise kept Sophie too busy to notice the speculative glances.

By the end of the meal, after numerous touching speeches, toasts and roasts, everyone in the room was buzzed on excellent food and fine wine, and Sophie was talking and laughing with his friends as if she'd known them for years. He'd never seen her this way before. He'd only ever seen her in work mode, cool and focused, or else alone with him.

He could just stare for hours, but people would notice. Hell, they already had.

Sophie looked as if she belonged in the wedding party. He wished he could enjoy himself as much as she seemed to, but Bryce's scheming made him tense.

He felt cheated. He was in a beautiful place, surrounded by the people he loved most in the world, in the company of the most sexy, fascinating woman he'd ever encountered.

It would have been perfect, if someone hadn't been trying to prove that his new lover was a liar, a thief and a spy. And warning her about it would only make it worse.

No matter how he sliced it, it felt like betrayal.

Sophie was surprised at how much fun she was having. This was her first real opportunity to observe Ava and Drew Maddox at close range, and she liked them. Ava and Jenna made a big effort to draw her out, and she let them do it.

Everyone was so warm and welcoming. They really seemed to care about each other. And she had more in common with her cousins than she'd thought. They were all orphans, since Drew and Ava had lost their parents in a plane crash when they were in their teens. But Malcolm had looked after them, in his gruff, clumsy way, and they had turned out fine. It seemed like a wonderful family to belong to.

She wondered if that would change if she came forward with her claim. If they would close ranks against her. It was a painful thought and hard to imagine now, with everyone so relaxed and happy because of the wedding.

Except for Vann, for some reason. Vann was unusually quiet, and his expression was grim. As the dinner began to wind down, and people started pushing their chairs back to leave, Drew stood up.

"Public service announcement, everyone," he said. "Jenna and I arranged for perfect weather for you all. The moon's almost full, there's no rain and not much wind. Perfect night for a walk on the beach. That's where we'll be. You're welcome."

Jenna stood, and the two of them came together in a swift, intense kiss. Then they waved at the crowd and strolled together, arms around each other's waists, out the dining room exit onto the terrace outside.

Sophie caught that tormented look on Vann's face again. "Everything okay?"

"Sure," he replied. "Why wouldn't it be?"

"You tell me," she said. "You seem off tonight. Too quiet. And tense."

Vann drained his wineglass. "It's been a long day," he said tersely.

"Understood," Sophie said, standing up. "Go rest, then. See you in the morning."

He caught her wrist as she started to leave the table. "Wait. Where are you going?"

"To the beach. I've never walked on a beach on this side of the Pacific before."

"Not alone," he said.

"Oh, please," she said. "I bet almost everyone at this table apart from Malcolm will end up out there on the beach. It's perfectly safe. Go to bed. Don't trouble yourself."

"Hell, no," he said. "I'm going with you."

She rolled her eyes. "Fine, then. Suit yourself."

The terrace outside segued into a walkway leading to an observation deck that overlooked the sea cliffs. A staircase to the beach below was bolted to the cliff face. The gleaming expanse of wet sand was lapped by the wide, foamy waves, and broken at intervals by jagged humps and spires of black volcanic rock. There was a bright, eerie glow on the water as the almost full moon lit up the night.

Vann led her to the head of the stairway. "There's a wooden shelf here where you can leave your shoes," he said.

Sweet relief, to slip off her heels. Vann took off his own shoes, and they made their way down the sandy staircase, zigging and zagging until they reached the bottom.

Their feet sank into the cool, dry sand as they slowly worked their way over to the water. The foam was icy cold when it first rushed over Sophie's feet, and she gasped and laughed. Vann stopped to roll up the legs of his pants.

At some point, she stumbled on a rock that poked up out of the sand. Vann caught her arm to steady her, and his hand slipped down to clasp her fingers, squeezing them as the cold water had numbed away the pain of her stubbed toes.

The contact made the memories of their passionate night flare through her body, making her weak with fresh yearning. She tugged her hand free. "We can't."

"Why not?"

"Don't you dare play dumb," she said. "We've been through this. Your best friend is getting married. His uncle is your boss. Let's nix any potential drama and concentrate on what's important here, which is Drew's wedding."

"There's nothing shocking or dramatic about holding hands on a moonlit beach."

Sophie took a step away from him. "Depends on the context. And the audience."

They looked around. As Sophie had predicted, several people had taken Drew and Jenna's suggestion. The happy couple were a tiny bit farther up on the beach. They were madly kissing each other, not caring who saw.

Lucky them.

"What would it take to get us to the point where we could hold hands on a beach?" Vann demanded. He sounded almost angry.

Sophie's chin went up. "We'd have to do the work," she said. "It's not instant. It's not automatic. You know, the way sex can be sometimes. Maybe that was a mistake."

"No," he said. "That was the farthest thing from a mistake I ever felt."

"Nice to hear, but even so," Sophie said. "We'd need transformation before hand-holding on a beach could happen. We'd have to make some big choices. Come to some conclusions about things. Otherwise, nothing. So stop it. You're bugging me tonight."

"I didn't mean to piss you off," Vann said.

"It's fine." She turned her back on him and walked away.

Vann trailed along behind her for a while before catching up and walking next to her again. The silence was starting to weigh on her, so she threw out a conversation opener as a peace offering.

"Your friends seem wonderful," she commented. "What a fun group of people."

"Yes, they are. I'm lucky. Drew and Zack are like brothers to me. Not that I had brothers as a kid, but I like to imagine it would be like my relationship with them."

"I have good friends like that, but they're scattered all over the world," she said. "One's still in Singapore, one is in Hong Kong, one got married to a guy from Sydney. A couple of them are in Europe. I never see them all together. And I hardly ever see any of them face-to-face. Just phone calls, or Skype."

"That's tough," he said. "It must be lonely."

Sophie didn't reply. For a moment, she couldn't trust her own voice. Her throat felt hot and soft. Admitting to loneliness was taking this instant intimacy a little too far. She didn't want him to feel sorry for her.

She turned away from him, staring out at the streak of moonlight on the sea and the surges of surf. They'd almost reached the end of this expanse of beach, and were coming to a more jagged, rocky place full of tide pools. Without a word, they turned and started back the way they came. They were quiet this time, but she was intensely aware of Vann's tall, brooding presence. The water boiled and frothed around her toes and ankles. The salty breeze whipped her skirt and lifted her hair like a banner.

His spell was working on her again. Being out in the infinite hugeness of this beautiful place…it fed that part of her that yearned for freedom, wildness. The same part of her that hungered for Vann. His power, his energy. His sexual generosity.

Sophie climbed back up the many long flights of steps that hugged the cliff side. Her shoes had gone clammy and sticky in the humid sea air, so she didn't bother putting them back on her sandy feet, but just walked down the wooden walkway barefoot.

Vann walked her to the door of her cabin. "Wait," he said as she reached for her key card.

"What?"

"Look at this. For sandy feet." Vann stepped on a small wooden pallet placed near the stepstone, and grabbed a small, retractable spray hose coiled up there.

He rinsed the sand off his own feet, and then gestured for her to step on the pallet.

Once she did so, Vann aimed the stream of cool water over her feet.

It was yet another one of his seductive tricks. The rush of cool water was soothing. He brushed the sticky sand off, caressing her feet with his hands.

The contact made her speechless and flustered. She fumbled for her key card. Fumbled again as she tried to find the switch that turned on the lights. Vann waited silently outside the door.

She turned around and beckoned impatiently for him to enter. "Oh, just get in here before someone sees you lurking."

He came inside and shut the door, but didn't walk into the room. "You're still mad at me," he said.

"Yes," she said. "Because you're still sulking. And you won't tell me why."

"Do you want me to leave?" he asked.

"No," she said. "I want to know what the hell your problem is. So I can understand if it's fixable or not."

"I'm not sure what you mean." His voice was guarded.

She flapped her hand at him angrily. "You're different tonight. All wound up. Negative. You weren't like that last night, so what's changed?"

He shook his head. "I don't know. I'm sorry if I'm pissing you off."

She waited for more, then shook her head in frustration. "You can't say what's wrong?"

"No," he said. "Sorry. I don't know what else to say."

She tried to read his face, but it was an impenetrable mask. "Did I say or do something that bothered you?"

"Not at all," he said. "You're perfect."

She snorted. "Hardly that. Then what is it?"

He turned toward the door. "I think I'd better go."

"Stop it," she snapped. "I already told you to come in. I want you here, but not the whole night. I don't want people seeing you leave in the morning, and have to deal with the snickering and the side-eye. I'm at a disadvantage here as it is. Understand?"

He set his shoes down. "As you command."

She gave him a narrow look. "Are you making fun of me?"

"Hell, no," he said. "I wouldn't dare."

Sophie put her hands on her hips. "Before anything else happens," she said. "Let's discuss a couple logistical details. We got carried away last night, and we never talked about safe sex. I trust you have more condoms with you?"

"Only one. I didn't have a chance to buy more. But I'll make that one count."

"You'd better," she said. "But while we're talking about this, I'll take this opportunity to tell you that I haven't been with anyone for a long time, and I've had bloodwork done since then. I'm disease free. Just so you know."

"Thanks for bringing it up, and so am I," he told her. "I always use condoms. I get tested regularly, and I've been tested since the last time I was involved with someone."

Sophie bit her lip thoughtfully as she weighed the risks and temptations. He did not strike her as dishonest. By no means. Moody, yes. Mysterious, yes. But not a liar.

"In that case, shall we dispense with the latex?" she said, her voice tentative. "I have a contraceptive implant, and it's good for another year or so."

Vann's throat worked. "Whoa," he muttered. "That would be…incredible. I would love it. I'm honored that you trust me that much."

"I haven't done that with anyone, ever," she told him. "I never wanted to risk it before. But tonight, for some reason, I do."

"Thank you," he said.

They gazed at each other in a moment of confused shyness.

Sophie shook it off with some difficulty. "So, Vann," she said. "Since yesterday's adventure started with me naked and you fully clothed, let's switch it up. Your turn, buddy. Strip. Let's see your stuff."

Vann's lips twitched, but he undressed quickly. Shirt, belt, pants. In moments, he stood there, stark naked, and ready to play from the looks of his stiff erection.

He reached out, sliding the silk jacket off her shoulders. "Your turn," he said.

He took his time with peeling off the close-fitting knit top. He explored the contours of the balcony-lace demi bra that propped up her bosom, his thumb sliding across her nipple, taut and dark against the lace. He slid his hands to her waist and sank down to his knees, pressing his face against her belly. The warmth of his breath heated the chiffon fabric of her skirt. He stroked his big, hot hands slowly up her legs beneath her skirt. Hooking her panties, he eased them down.

She stepped out of them, gasping as he pushed the front of her skirt up and pressed his face against her. Kissing, caressing, opening her with lips and tongue.

She watched the shockingly intimate scene in the mirror. Her in just her skirt and bra, him naked on his knees, her skirt bunched up at her belly as he pleasured her. The back view of him would have taken her breath away if she had any breath to take.

She clutched his shoulders, swaying on her feet, panting with shocked delight at the tender swirl and flick of his tongue against her most sensitive flesh. She wound her fingers into his warm hair as the wild sensations lifted her—and then sent her flying.

Vann was on his feet, holding her steady. She barely noticed as he peeled the rest of her clothes off. She just felt gravity shifting and was aware of being lifted. Then cool sheets pressed against her back, and his scorching heat came down next to her.

"Wait," she said.

He went still, eyes narrowed. "Yeah? What for?"

"You lie down on your back," she said. "I want to look at you."

He rolled over, head propped on the pillow. She feasted her eyes on that gorgeously strong male body, draped lazily across the bed. He held his stiff erection in his hand. He stroked it slowly as he smiled, his dark, sultry bedroom eyes saying, *Come and get it. If you dare.*

His self-assurance aroused her. Without ever seeming arrogant, he had complete confidence that he could please her. He instinctively knew how.

It switched her on like nothing ever had.

Sophie clambered over him, swinging her leg over his until she had him right where she needed him. She slowly took him inside…undulating, rising and falling, until the pleasure surged up, hot and sweet and wrenching.

When she came back up for air, Vann had rolled her

over onto her back, folding her legs high. He propped himself up on his elbows as he once again pushed inside her clinging warmth and began to move. Surging, rocking. She was so primed, after what had come before. Slick and soft and sensitized. Every slow, gliding thrust made her whimper with delight.

The bed shook as their rhythm quickened. Sophie writhed, digging her nails into him, goading him on. That hugeness was opening up in her mind again, the endless space and power that she'd felt on the beach with the stars and the sky and the sea. Wild magic, wild mystery. Pleasure exploding, flinging them into that enormous nowhere together.

Sophie floated in the glow of residual pleasure. When she opened her eyes, she turned to look at Vann with a lazy, satiated smile.

He didn't smile back.

He almost looked like he was bracing himself.

A chill settled into her, someplace very deep.

She tried to breathe down the hurt, but she had no barriers right now. Her walls were down, but he'd kept his own walls as high as ever. That hurt.

Be a grown-up, she lectured herself. He'd made no promises to her. This was just a fun, hot thing for him. Women must throw themselves at him all the time.

She was the one making it stupid by getting all emotional. Like a shivering virgin falling like a ton of bricks for the first guy who ever touched her.

She was careful to keep her tone light. "There you go again. All down in the mouth. What is it with you tonight, Vann?"

Vann shook his head, but he didn't deny it. "I can't seem to shake it."

Sophie rolled onto her back and stared at the ceiling. "If what just happened can't make you feel better, nothing will," she said. "If you're so miserable, why are you here?"

"Because I'm starving for more," he said. "Because I never want it to stop."

She was taken aback by his stark intensity. And confused. "You just got more," she said slowly. "A lot more. And you've still got that sad look on your face."

Vann clapped his hand over his eyes. "I'm sorry," he ground out. "There's nothing I can do about it. I can't control the way I feel. It just happens."

"I understand." Sophie slid off the bed. "That settles it. Go sulk in your own room. That was hot and fabulous, but we're done, Vann. Like always, it's been real."

"Sophie—"

"I'm getting into the shower. When I'm out, I want the room to myself."

"I didn't mean to make you angry."

"You say you can't control the way you feel. Well, neither can I. Good night."

She made it into the bathroom just in time and set the shower running, hand pressed to her quivering lips. She welcomed the hot spray coming down on her face.

She wished she could wash away those inconvenient feelings. Be empty and free of them. Then the shower door creaked. A rush of cool air kissed her skin.

Vann stepped inside with her. His big body took up all the space, making the huge shower stall suddenly feel cramped. She dashed water from her face, and opened her mouth to tell him to back the hell off—and then she saw his eyes. Pain he couldn't express.

She recognized that nameless pain. She'd felt it herself. "Vann—"

He cut her off with a kiss. It was too sweet and too hot to resist.

Vann hit the faucet to switch the shower off. In the steamy, dripping quiet she could hear her own heart thudding in her ears, her own breathless, helpless whimpering gasps. The sounds of absolute sensual surrender.

He spun her around, placing her hands flat against the wall, and then pulled her hips back and nudged her feet apart. She opened to him, arching her back as he reached around with his hand to expertly caress her as he sank his thick shaft slowly inside her.

She rocked back, trying to take him deeper, but he kept his surging rhythm slow and relentless. The heavy, gliding thrusts were delicious, each one stoking her excitement until she wanted to claw and scream at him.

He finally gave in to her demands and moved faster, harder, rising to meet the power building up inside her.

She cried out as the intense sensations raging through her body wiped her out.

Vann stayed inside her afterward, his face pressed to her neck. He bit her shoulder gently, then tenderly licked the spot. "I know I was supposed to go," he said. "I just can't seem to pry myself away."

"You are the master of mixed signals, you know that?"

"I know," he said. "I'm sorry."

"I'm sick of your apologizing," she said. "Go back to your room now."

"Do I have to?"

"Yes," she said. "There are some definitions to get

straight. There's scenario A, a secret workplace affair. That's a specific set of rules and expectations. Then there's scenario B, a boyfriend. Totally different rules and expectations. You're mixing them up. You're not my boyfriend. Don't act like you are. That's a whole other level of intimacy."

"This feels pretty intimate to me," he said.

She squirmed out of his grip, and turned the water back on, soaping herself up without looking at him. "My job is important to me," she said. "Don't threaten it."

"I never meant to," he said.

She met his eyes. "You're pushing too hard. I need a break. I'll see you at breakfast. Good night, Vann. Off you go."

Vann didn't look at her as he toweled off and left the bathroom. Something inside her snapped when she heard the cabin door close a couple of minutes later. Alone at last, just like she'd insisted.

She promptly fell to pieces.

Thirteen

Vann had to stop himself from jumping up to get Sophie's attention at breakfast. He had to abide by the rules. But the rules felt like a jacket that was two sizes too small.

"Sophie! There you are!" Jenna called out. "I was wondering where you were."

Sophie gave Jenna a smile as she approached the table where Vann sat with Ava, Drew, Zack and the bride-to-be. She looked amazing, in a stretchy sunshine-yellow top that wrapped smoothly over her breasts and showed off her narrow waist, and wide-legged white linen pants. Her hair was still down. He could smell her fresh scent from across the table.

A stern glance from Sophie told him he was staring. He looked away.

"Good morning," Sophie said, smiling at Drew and

Jenna. “I see the weather is holding for you. My phone told me it’s going to be sunny and warm this afternoon.”

“I know, right? And the beach last night was wonderful,” Ava said. Her curious gaze flicked from Sophie to Vann, but thankfully, Sophie didn’t seem to notice as she sat down. “Did you sleep in?”

“No, I’ve just been running around, getting organized,” Sophie said. “I went to see when Mr. Zhang might need me. His grandson tells me that Malcolm and Hendrick have the conference room scheduled for eleven. That gives me plenty of time for breakfast.”

“Good,” Ava said. “Relax and enjoy. I hear Uncle Malcolm was doing his best Dickensian supervillain routine down in San Francisco. He’s so annoying when he does that.”

She shrugged. “It wasn’t that bad. I lived.”

“We’re glad you did,” Jenna told her. “Fuel up. We’ve got a long day of celebrating ahead of us.”

“Hey, Richard,” said Ava with a bright smile. “How nice to see you again!”

Vann glanced up and saw Richard Bryce standing there. He’d met Tim’s son a couple of other times over the years. Richard was a tall, good-looking man with a buzz cut and a neatly trimmed beard. From the way Richard looked at Sophie, Vann suspected that Bryce had already shared his suspicions about her with his son.

Then again, any guy could be excused for staring at Sophie.

But then Richard slid into the seat opposite Sophie and proceeded to talk her ear off as she ate her breakfast, trying to impress her with his clout as a budding

Hollywood mogul. As the minutes passed, all desire to be charitable and understanding with Richard Bryce swirled down the drain.

"Yeah, it's intense," Rich was saying to Ava. "There are always at least a hundred people ready to stab me in the back so they can take my job. I have to stay on my toes."

"Hmm," Sophie murmured. "Sounds stressful. Do you like the work at least?"

"God, yes," Rich said. "It's what I was born for." As Rich spoke, his eyes drifted down to Sophie's chest. "I've won six awards in the last two years. I get offers from headhunters every day. People try to poach me all the time."

"That's great, Rich," Ava said. "I'm so glad it's working out for you."

Rich turned his attention to Sophie. "Everyone in this crowd is in the wedding party except for you and me," he said. "Let's leave them to it and go down to the beach until it's time for the ceremony. There are some amazing tide pools I'd love to show you."

"She's working," Vann said. "Interpreting for Malcolm and Hendrick."

Rich blinked at him, as if startled to realize that Vann existed. His smile widened. "Ah! Dude, I get it. My apologies. I didn't mean to move in on your territory."

"Not at all," Sophie said. "No territory here. And I can speak for myself." She gave Vann a sharp look. "But it's true," she said to Rich. "I'm busy this morning."

"Well, all right. Looks like you all have lots to do,

so I'll just get out of your hair." Rich got up. "See you at the ceremony."

After Rich was halfway across the room, Ava smacked her forehead with the heel of her hand and glared at Drew. "Remind me why you invited him?"

Drew shrugged. "Uncle Malcolm insisted. To make Tim Bryce happy, I guess? Tim is convinced that Rich and I were the best of friends all through our tender boyhood. You know. Childhood memories, summers on the lake and all that?"

Ava snorted. "Yeah, him constantly trying to undo the strings of my bikini top," she said. "He was a bra-snapping dweeb back then, and surprise, surprise, he still is."

"Ignore him," Drew said. "We've all got better things to think about."

"We certainly do." Ava turned a misty look on Jenna. "I still can't believe it. My two favorite people in the world, coming together. It's a dream come true."

Ava and Jenna dissolved into tears and wrapped each other in a big, sniffling hug. Sophie caught Vann's eye. "I should go get ready for Malcolm and Mr. Zhang," she said.

"I'll walk you to the conference room," Vann said.

"You're drawing attention to us," Sophie said as they walked through the dining room.

"I'm just walking beside you," he said under his breath. "I'm not touching you. Surely that's not suspicious. We're colleagues, right?"

"And fending off that guy at the breakfast table? What was that all about?"

He shrugged defensively. "He pissed me off. Tide pools, my ass."

"I don't need protection," Sophie told him. "I'm capable of decimating any man who gives me unwanted attention with no help from you. You're acting like a jealous boyfriend, and it's visible from miles away. Please, stop it."

Vann stopped in the corridor. "I can't get anything right with you."

"Not if you draw attention to us in public like that," she said crisply. "I know the way to the conference room. I'll take it from here. Later, Vann."

As Sophie walked away, he stood there, stung.

Banished to the doghouse.

Malcolm, Hendrick and Zhang discussed the Nairobi Towers project for well over two hours before a knock finally sounded on the door.

Ava poked her head in, giving the men a brilliant smile. "I hate to interrupt you gentlemen, but just a heads-up. The ceremony is in two hours, and Bev sent me to nudge you." She winked at Hendrick. "So blame her and not me. She wants everything to run on time."

"Bev is, as always, the ultimate authority," Malcolm said, his voice surprisingly jovial as he snapped the laptop shut. "We can continue tomorrow, I suppose. Don't keep your wife waiting, Hendrick."

After the men left the conference room, Sophie hurried back to her room to look through her much depleted wardrobe. The choice was clear. The last dress standing.

She slipped on the dusty-rose dress. It was bias-cut silk chiffon with a long, filmy wrap. The underdress faded from dark on the clinging bodice to light at the skirt, and the wrap was a couple of shades lighter, with a loose, floppy chiffon rose at the hooked closure. She put on her spike-heeled strappy sandals made of black velvet, and freshened her makeup. Then she transferred phone, tissues and room card to her beaded evening bag with a chiffon rose that matched the wrap.

And that was it. She'd done all she could.

At least the bride and groom in question were incredibly sweet about her crashing their wedding. She hoped that someday she'd be able to claim those people as friends. Maybe even family. A girl could hope, but hope was a risky enterprise. The chance of this going sour was very high.

With Vann. With the Maddoxes. She had to stay chill, or she could hurt herself.

She'd tried to tame her hair with the blow dryer and the curling iron, but the minute she stepped outside, the wind whipped it around madly. The wedding was to be held out on a relatively sheltered swath of lawn in the lee of a big rocky outcropping near the reception hall of the resort. Beyond the lawn, the turf segued into waist-deep fields of wildflowers that covered the rest of the countryside.

Once she got there, the worst of the wind would be blocked, but her hair was already a casualty.

The day was warm for spring on the coast. She was fine in the clingy sleeveless dress and the filmy chiffon wrap. As she drew near to the main building, a woman came out, dressed in the tailored maroon jacket and black trousers of the resort staff.

It was Julie, she realized. The woman spotted her and hurried in her direction, her ponytail bobbing wildly.

"Ms. Valente! I'm so glad I caught you!" she called out. "I called your room, but you must have just left!"

"You're looking for me?" Sophie asked. "Why?"

"Mr. Maddox needs you urgently, for a quick interpretation job," Julie said. "You're supposed to go to his room immediately."

"Now?" Sophie glanced at her watch. "But…the wedding's about to begin."

"I know! Which is why you have to hurry! The room number is 156, the Madrone Suite." Julie held out a brochure with a map. She'd scribbled with a ballpoint pen to mark the way, and circled cabin 156. "See? It's this big one, at the end of the main walkway."

Sophie took the brochure, still perplexed. "Are you sure—"

"Absolutely! You'd better hurry. You don't want to hold them up."

"Okay. Thanks for telling me."

Sophie was tempted to take off her shoes to run back to Malcolm's cabin. She'd certainly make better time. But she didn't want to spend the day with sand between her toes.

The walkways were deserted. The timing was strange but Malcolm Maddox was the boss. Maybe he was so eccentric and egoistic he figured everyone and everything could wait upon his pleasure. Including his nephew's wedding.

Still, what on earth could be urgent enough for such a delay?

Whatever. It was not her call, nor was it her problem. She was just a lackey, so she'd do her job and shut up about it. But damn, the wind was tossing her hair around. She was going to look like she'd been flying through a storm on a broomstick by the time she got back to the ceremony. She spotted the cabin up ahead, peeked at her watch and half ran on the balls of her feet to the door. She knocked.

She waited for a moment for a response, then knocked again. "Mr. Maddox?" she called. "Are you in there?"

No response. The seconds ticked by. She tried again, knocking for the third time, loudly enough so that it might seem rude to anyone inside. He was an old man, but she hadn't gotten the impression that he was hard of hearing. "Mr. Maddox?" she yelled. "Are you in there?"

Could he be in the bathroom? Or, God forbid, having some kind of health emergency? But she had no way to go inside and check on him.

The best thing would be to run like hell back to the main hall and let someone else know that Malcolm was in his room, but not responding. So he could get help.

She checked her watch again, shoving her hair back impatiently, and trotted back the way she came as quickly as she could. Hoping that everything was okay with Malcolm.

When she got to the main building, she was in a cold sweat, scared for him.

She could see the crush of the wedding party through the picture window at the end of the building, the tents and streamers.

Then she saw Malcolm there, clutching his cane. Jenna was on his arm. He was starting up the grassy aisle with slow, halting steps. Giving away the bride.

He'd never been in his room at all. What the *hell*? So this Julie character had sent her on a fool's errand.

The directions were too specific to be a mistake. Was it some sort of lame prank?

She turned around, fuming, and went to the front desk. "Excuse me," she said to the woman behind the desk. "Could you put me in touch with your colleague Julie?"

The woman gave her a blank look. "Um, who?"

Sophie's patience was at the breaking point. Her voice got louder. "Julie? Short, blond ponytail? She just sent me off to my boss's room and told me he was waiting for me there. But he wasn't, because he's outside right now, giving away the bride. I really need to talk to her and find out what the hell just happened."

The woman, whose name tag read "Debra," looked frightened. "Ah, ma'am… I'm supersorry, but I don't know what you mean. We don't have a Julie on our staff."

Sophie stared at her, mouth open. "Excuse me?"

"We have a Gina and a Jennifer," Debra said. "And a Julian, on the maintenance staff, but he's a man in his sixties."

"But I saw…but she had a name tag like yours," Sophie said blankly. "She wore the uniform. She knew my name, and that I worked for Mr. Maddox. How is that possible?"

"I have no idea, ma'am. I promise you, I have absolutely no idea," Debra said. "I've never met a Julie since I've been here, and this is my third year. Do you want me to call the general manager? Maybe she can tell you something more."

Sophie was opening her mouth to say yes, by all means, do call the general manager, when a voice from behind made her jump.

"Sophie! What are you doing here? The ceremony's already begun!" It was Rich Bryce, poking his head inside the door. "Aren't you coming out?"

"Ah…sure. I'm just confused. Someone told me to meet Mr. Maddox in his room just now. But when I got there—"

"Meet Malcolm? Any fool knew that he'd be here, giving away the bride."

"I know," Sophie said through her teeth. "But—"

"It must have been some kind of mix-up. Come on, or we'll miss the whole thing."

Sophie glanced back at the wide-eyed Debra. "After the wedding, I would like to speak to your general manager. Would you let her know I want a meeting?"

"Of course! I'll let her know right away," Debra assured her. "I'm so sorry!"

Rich took her by the arm, pulling her so abruptly she tottered on her heels. Sophie jerked her arm back. "I'll walk at my own pace, thanks," she said frostily.

Rich lifted his hands with an apologetic grin. "Sorry. It's just that you're late."

"Don't concern yourself," she said. "It's my problem, not yours."

But Rich wasn't easy to shake. He followed on her heels as she made her way across the wide swath of green lawn to the crowd.

Rich took her arm as she stepped onto the grass. She snatched it away again. She was forced to pull so hard the gesture was evident to everyone around them.

Sophie joined the edge of the big crowd and Rich took up a position uncomfortably close to her, the front of his body touching the back of hers, forcing her to inch forward again and again. Their position suggested that they were together.

As-freaking-if. She edged away. He oozed after her. This was all her reputation needed, now that people had noticed the energy between her and Vann. Showing up late for the wedding trailing yet another man in her wake? Just call her the Harlot of Maddox Hill.

And, of course, Vann's gaze locked on to her the second she was in his line of vision. He had a perfect view up there on the raised dais, flanking Drew along with Zack, and looking absolutely smashing in his tux. Malcolm had brought Jenna up the aisle, and had gone back to the front row to sit down next to Bev and Hendrick.

Jenna and her bridesmaids took their places. The bride looked stunning in her white lace and long train, holding a bouquet of wildflowers, her hair a curly strawberry blond cloud crowned with yet more flowers. She was followed by Ava and Cherise, both looking great in clinging midnight-blue wrap dresses. Cherise's bionic arm was decorated with blinking lights of every shade of blue. The ring bearer, a preteen Arm's Reach client Sophie had met at the dinner last night, was holding a pillow with two rings pinned to it, a big smile on his face.

Sophie slid between two of the other guests to put space between herself and Rich, but it didn't work. Rich just shamelessly elbowed them out of the way to reclaim his place beside her, to the accompaniment of hissing and muttered complaints.

The only way to get away from him was to be harsh,

bitchy and loud. To make a big, unattractive spectacle of herself and risk marring the wedding.

What a way to endear herself to her new cousins.

Fourteen

Zack nudged Vann's arm. He'd zoned out during his best friend's wedding, first wondering where the hell Sophie was, then wondering why in holy hell she'd ended up coming out so late, and in the company of that asshat Rich Bryce.

He dragged his attention back to the celebrant, who was saying something sentimental about mutual trust. Jenna and Drew had that drunk-on-happiness look that used to make him nervous and uncomfortable, and now just made him envious.

Nervous and uncomfortable had been preferable.

He was going to schedule a meeting with Hendrick and Malcolm as soon as possible when they were back in Seattle on Tuesday. Lay it all out for them. He wanted to take this relationship with Sophie to the next level.

And he wasn't going to let Bryce's bullshit hold him back.

The crowd erupted in cheers and applause. Drew and Jenna were kissing passionately. When they came up for air, they beamed at each other.

Zack nudged him again. Time to process out after the new bride and groom. They'd practiced the choreography after breakfast, but it was all gone from his head.

Zack and Ava went first, and then Cherise took the lead, grabbing his arm and towing him along after them.

Sophie looked at him intently as he passed, as if she were trying to tell him something with her eyes, but he couldn't grasp what it was, not with Rich Bryce hanging over her with that self-satisfied look on his face, like he'd gotten away with something.

Postwedding chaos followed. Tears, showers of flower petals and eco-friendly bird feed over the bride. A crush of wedding guests descended on the receiving line.

He couldn't find Sophie in all the hubbub afterward, but he kept looking.

He finally found her on one of the cliff overlooks. She'd gotten a glass of champagne, and was gazing out on the surf as she sipped it.

Vann grabbed a glass from a passing waiter's tray and joined her. "There you are."

She gave him a guarded smile and lifted her glass. "Well, they did it. Beautiful ceremony."

"It was," he said, clinking it with his own. "To Jenna and Drew."

They drank, and leaned their elbows on the railing, gazing out at the sea together.

"Where were you when the ceremony started?" he asked.

Sophie shook her head. "It was the strangest thing," she said. "I was on my way there, but right when I got to the door of the reception hall, this woman dressed like hotel staff told me that Malcolm urgently needed me in his hotel room."

"What?"

"I know, right? She said he needed me to interpret. The timing seemed bizarre, but she was very insistent, so I just hightailed it up there and knocked on his door. But he wasn't there. Of course, because he was here all along. Obviously. The wedding was about to start. Which means that someone was jerking me around. So I hurried back, and asked at the desk to speak to the person who's sent me on this fool's errand—Julie's her name. And the woman tells me there is no Julie on the resort staff. Never has been in the three years she's worked here."

"That is bizarre," Vann said.

"I know," Sophie agreed fervently. "And it's not the first time I saw her. She was in my room last night when we got here. She'd delivered my bags while we were in that meeting with Tim. She said she dropped my garment bag and got it wet, so she was laying my clothes out on the bed. Now they tell me this person I've interacted with twice never worked here? It gives me the shivers."

Vann shook his head. "I don't like the sound of it."

"Me, neither. I'm hesitant to talk to the general manager about it now. Out of embarrassment. It sounds… weird. Like I'm delusional. Or seeing ghosts."

"You're as solid as a rock," he assured her. "Trust yourself. I certainly do."

She gave him a grateful smile. "Thanks. I appreciate your faith in my sanity."

"So, ah…" he said after a moment's silence. "How is it that you ended up arriving at the ceremony with Rich Bryce?"

Vann had kept his voice neutral, but Sophie still gave him a withering look. "For real, you are asking me that?"

"Just wondering," he said innocently.

"I ran across him in the resort lobby when I was asking about this mysterious Julie, if you must know," she said. "He attached himself to me like a leech. I literally had to pry him loose a couple times. So don't waste my time being jealous about that guy. I have far more urgent problems. He does not even make the cut. Clear?"

Vann felt his chest relax. "Crystal clear. Shall I kick his ass?"

"Not funny," she said. "I want no more drama. Spectral hotel staff are more than enough stress for me to deal with."

"Oh, so that's where you two are hiding!" Ava broke in after bursting out the door of the reception hall. Her blond hair was tousled around her flushed, beautiful face. "Come back in! Bev and Malcolm are about to start speechifying. You guys can whisper and canoodle later."

Busted. He shot Sophie a guilty glance, but she ignored him as she followed Ava inside, her skirt fluttering in the breeze.

* * *

It was strange. In spite of all her issues, plus the mysterious, disappearing Julie, Sophie was actually having a good time. The happiness around her was infectious. Drew and Jenna were ecstatic to be married to each other, and everyone else basked in the reflected glory.

The party had a natural momentum. Everything was beautiful. The surroundings were gorgeous, the food was fabulous and abundant, the wine was excellent and the music was amazing. The band played three long and very danceable sets, and the music was a perfect blend of high-energy pieces to get everyone dancing and heart-melting romantic ballads.

Sophie didn't usually dance, but she couldn't say no when Ava dragged her out onto the floor to be part of a chorus line. It left her breathless and damp and pink, and intensely aware of Vann watching from the table where he sat with Zack.

"Single ladies, single ladies! All the single ladies gather around!"

Oh, no, no, no. Bev Hill was on the warpath. Hendrick's wife was the honorary benevolent matriarch of this event, since both Drew's and Jenna's mothers were gone. She was hustling around, rousting out the unmarried women and herding them into the center of the room. No way was Sophie getting roped into the bouquet toss.

Sophie tried to melt out of sight, but Bev swung around and pointed an accusing finger at her. "And just where do you think you're going, young lady?"

"Oh, no. Not me," Sophie protested. "I'm only here

in a professional capacity. I wasn't even invited to this wedding. So I certainly shouldn't participate in the—"

"Nonsense. You just get your patootie right out here with the other girls," Bev directed. "This only counts if everybody plays along. Come on, now!"

So it was that Sophie found herself in the midst of twenty sweaty, giggling young woman, all high on dancing and champagne. They were herded into a tight formation, she and Ava shooting each other commiserating glances as Bev jockeyed Jenna into position.

The rest of the crowd ringed the group, laughing and cheering them on as Jenna positioned herself, turned around…and flung her bouquet high into the air.

It arced, turning and spinning…right toward Sophie's head.

She put up her hand to shield her face. It bounced off her fingers like a volleyball, and then thudded down onto her chest, where she caught it instinctively. Oh, God. No.

The room erupted in riotous cheers.

"Woo-hoo! You're next," Ava shouted over the din. "Good luck with that!"

Sophie couldn't reply, being thronged with hugs and squeals and teasing best wishes.

Vann kept his distance during the ordeal, thank God, but he'd watched the whole thing. She was too self-conscious to go near where he was sitting, so she let Bev lead her over to a table where Ava and Jenna were resting their feet.

She sat down gratefully. There was a steep price to be paid for dancing in high-heeled sandals. She needed a break from the implacable force of gravity right about now.

Bev pulled a bottle of champagne out of the ice bucket and poured them all fresh chilled glasses. "Drink up, hon! Fate has chosen you to be next."

Sophie couldn't hold back the snort. "Fate may have a rude surprise in store," she said. "I'm a tough nut to crack."

"Nonsense." Bev patted her hand. "A gorgeous young thing like you must have the suitors lined up out the door."

"It's never easy, Bev," Jenna reminded her.

"I suppose you're right," Bev admitted. "My romance with Hendrick was rather rocky at first. He was quite the bad boy, back in the day."

"Hendrick?" Sophie repeated, disbelieving. "A bad boy?"

Bev, Ava and Jenna burst out laughing at the tone of her voice.

"Yes!" Bev said. "Believe it or not, Hendrick was quite the player. I had to treat him very, very badly for a while. But I got him in line. Elaine helped me with that. Drew and Ava's mother. She was the one who got us together, forty-six years ago. She's been gone for over eighteen years now, and I still miss her so much."

Sophie looked from the rounded little lady with her white pixie cut, eyes dreamy behind her rimless glasses, over to the bald, tight-lipped Hendrick, sitting at a table with Malcolm, the elder Mr. Zhang and his grandson. Hendrick was leaning his good ear to hear young Zhang's interpretation, scowling in concentration. It was hard to imagine him as a focus of romance, but Bev's eyes were misty with sentimental memories.

"Congratulations," Sophie said. "On forty-six years

of happiness." She looked over at Jenna, and lifted her glass. "May you be just as lucky."

They drank, and Bev pulled out a tissue and dabbed at the tears leaking from below her glasses. She grabbed Jenna's hand. "This was Elaine's engagement ring," she told Sophie, lifting Jenna's hand. "Doesn't it just look perfect on her?"

Sophie admired the night-blue sapphire, nested in a cluster of small diamonds, that adorned Jenna's slender hand. "It is lovely."

"I can just feel Elaine's presence here tonight." Bev's voice was tear-choked. "She would have been so happy to see Drew with you. She was so proud of her children."

Ava dug into her purse for a tissue and mopped up her own eyes. "I should have worn waterproof mascara. What was I thinking?"

"Oh, honey, I didn't mean to make you cry."

"It's okay, Bev," Ava said. "It's just that I actually felt her, you know? Just a flash of her. It's been such a long time. I was afraid that I'd forgotten the way she made me feel forever. But I haven't. And you helped me remember."

Bev scooted closer and grabbed Ava in a tight hug.

Then they all broke down in tears. Sophie's eyes stung, and her throat was so tight it ached.

She missed Mom so badly. Mom would have known just what to say to transform all the tears into cathartic laughter, but Sophie hadn't inherited that gift.

"Was Malcolm ever married?" Sophie asked after Bev had wiped her eyes and blown her nose.

"Briefly," Ava said. "To Aunt Helen. It only lasted

a few years. She got bored easily, if you know what I mean. Though Uncle Malcolm is anything but boring."

"No one really liked her." Bev's voice hardened. "We all knew it was a mistake. Sure enough, she ended up running off." She turned to Ava. "That was before you were born. Drew was just a toddler."

"And he never married again?" Sophie asked.

"He never wanted to risk it," Bev said sadly. "In spite of all the choices he had. And he could have had his pick. Oh, he had his adventures. Nothing serious, though. He left a trail of broken hearts in his wake. But all that's long past now."

Sophie looked over at Malcolm. She thought about Bev, and her forty-six-year marriage with Hendrick. Of her own mother, staring at the sunset on the terrace with her glass of wine, and her regrets.

Vicky Valente had been a one-man woman, just like Bev. She should have had what Bev had. Weddings and births and graduations and funerals and all the messy, complicated business in between. But fate had not been kind.

Sophie pushed her chair back and got up, babbling something incoherent to Ava, Jenna and Bev. They looked up, blinking back tears, calling after her as she left.

She didn't register what they said. They were probably asking if she was okay, or if there was anything they could do. But she wasn't okay. And there was nothing anyone could do.

She just had to get someplace private, before she disgraced herself.

Fifteen

Where the hell had Sophie run off to?

Vann excused himself and headed toward the door he'd seen her leave through. Once outside on the walkways, he caught a flutter of her dark pink skirt before the path turned and the foliage hid her from view.

People on the walkway stared as he ran by. A big guy in a tux sprinting down the wooden walkway at top speed must look strange.

He hit the branch in the path. One way led to Malcolm's room, and Bryce's baited trap, whatever it might be. The other way led to Sophie's cabin. He turned in that direction, only slowing down when he got there. He tried to get his breathing calmed down before he knocked.

"No housekeeping, please," Sophie called from inside.

Vann was so relieved he practically floated off the ground. "Sophie? It's Vann."

There was a long pause. "It's not a great time."

"Are you okay?"

"I'm fine. I just need to be alone. I'll catch up with you later."

"Please," he insisted. "Let me talk to you. Just for a minute."

The silence was endless. Finally, to his huge relief, the door opened a crack.

He pushed it open and went inside. Sophie was in there, standing with her back to him. "What's so important that it can't wait a few hours?" she asked.

He shut the door. "What's wrong?"

"Oh. That's why you're invading my privacy? Because you're curious?"

"Just concerned," he said.

She blew her nose loudly. "I didn't ask for your concern."

"Too bad," Vann said. "You're getting it, anyway. Please tell me what's wrong."

She turned to face him. Her wet topaz eyes blazed. "Fine," she said. "Here it is, Vann. The shocking truth. I miss my mom."

He had no idea how to respond to that. "Ah…"

"Yes, I know," she said. "And that's the sum total of what's going on in here. Happy now?"

"I wouldn't say happy," he said carefully. "What brought that on?"

Sophie fished another tissue out of the pack. "It was a sneak attack," she said, blowing her nose. "Bev was going on about how sad it was that Drew's mom couldn't be here for the wedding. Ava started to cry, then Jenna piled on, then Bev, too, and the whole thing just got out of hand. But I'm not part of their club, and I didn't feel comfortable indulging in a cry with them. So I bailed. My clever plan was to have my sobfest in the privacy of my own room, where nobody could see me or judge me or, God forbid, feel sorry for me. But no, it was not to be. I have to do it in front of you."

"Not part of the club?" he asked. "What club?"

"Oh, you know," she said impatiently. "The inner sanctum. The family circle. I'm just hired help. It didn't seem appropriate. But I just miss her so much…" Sophie pressed her hand to her mouth.

"I'm so sorry you can't have what you want," he said. "I wish I could change that."

"Me, too," she whispered. "Thanks for wanting to."

He had hesitated to touch her—she seemed so raw and charged with electricity—but the impulse was too strong now. He pulled her into his arms, and waited until the tension vibrating through her relaxed, and her soft weight settled against his chest.

After a few moments, she rubbed her eyes. "I'll ruin your shirt."

"I don't care," he said.

"Wow," she whispered. "That just blindsided me. It was so hard last year, losing her. It happened so fast. I thought I was handling it, and suddenly, kaboom. I fall to pieces."

"I think it's normal," he said. "Family gatherings, holidays, weddings. They can really slip past your guard."

"Exactly," Sophie said. "My guard is usually miles high. It's the organizing principle of my professional life, you know? That's what I do. I help people keep up their guard. But the last few days, my guard has been like Swiss cheese. And my mom is the biggest hole of all. She's the reason I'm here."

Vann waited for more, but Sophie stopped speaking.

She pulled away with an incoherent apology, and went into the bathroom and bent over the sink, splashing her face.

He followed her and slid his arms around her waist from behind as she straightened up, dabbing at her face with the towel.

"What does that mean? That your mom is the reason you're here?" he asked.

She wouldn't meet his eyes. "I told you, remember? That's why I moved to Seattle. I needed a fresh start after she was gone."

Vann waited for more. Sophie finally met his eyes in the mirror.

"What?" she demanded, almost angrily.

"You're always straight with me, so I have a good baseline reading on you for honesty," he said. "And this doesn't ring true. What is it about your mom?"

She made a frustrated sound. "You are all up in my face tonight, Vann."

"Yes," he said. "And I'm not backing down."

Sophie let out a sharp sigh. Her eyes looked almost defiant. "All right," she said. "Here goes nothing. If I tell you a secret, will you promise not to tell a soul?"

Vann felt himself go ice cold inside. He couldn't think of what to say. "Ah…"

Sophie laughed out loud. "Oh, my God, your face," she said. "Relax, Vann. I'm not confessing to murder or anything shocking."

"Even so, I can't make that promise blind," he said carefully. "How do I know what you'll say?"

Sophie sighed. "How about if I promise in advance that my secret will not compromise you morally? It will not sully your honor to keep my promise. It's just private, that's all."

He nodded. "I see."

"So? Do you promise?"

Vann let out a slow breath, and braced himself. "I promise."

Sophie spun inside the circle of his arms, and placed both her hands on his chest. She looked like she was working up her courage.

"Is this about your mother?" he prompted.

Sophie nodded. "She was the one who wanted me to go to Seattle," she said. "It was her dying wish for me to come here."

Vann waited for the rest, unable to breathe. "And why is that?"

Sophie raised her eyes to his. "Because Malcolm Maddox is my father."

Vann looked blank. Stunned. But not dismayed, which was heartening.

"Whoa," he whispered at last. "No way. For real?"

"Absolutely for real," she said. "I didn't even know myself until right before Mom died. She always put me off when I asked about my father. It was the one thing we ever fought about. But when she got her terminal diagnosis, she changed her mind."

"So, it's a sure thing? You know this for a fact?"

Sophie nodded. "Mom had an affair with Malcolm thirty years ago, in New York. It happened while he was working on the Phelps Pavilion. My mother was on the team working on the interiors. They had a wild affair, for just a couple of weeks. She fell madly in love with him."

"And she never told him about you?"

"She tried," Sophie said. "She went to his house in Seattle. His wife, Helen, met her at the door. She was mortified. She left, and she never came back."

Vann stared at her, fascinated. "Yeah. I can see the family resemblance, now that I'm looking for it. To Ava, to Drew, to Malcolm. It's in the shape of the eyes, the eyebrows. It's so obvious. I can't believe I didn't notice it before."

"So you believe me? You don't think I'm some grifter trying to con them?"

He looked shocked. "Hell, no. Why would you lie about a thing like this?"

She laughed at him. "Oh, come on, Vann. Malcolm is rich and famous in his field, and he was known to get around in his wild youth. He probably has paternity suit insurance, for God's sake. Not that it's in any way relevant. I'm not after his money, or any sort of notoriety. On the contrary."

"It would never occur to me that you were after Malcolm's money," Vann said. "If you wanted money, you'd go make it yourself. You have the skills."

"Well, thank you," Sophie said. "That's a lovely compliment. To tell you another secret, I actually inherited quite a considerable sum of money from my grandparents. ItalMarble made my grandfather a very rich man. So I would never need to bother Malcolm at all if money was all that I cared about."

"What do you care about?"

"It's hard to put my finger on," she said. "It was important to Mom. Fulfilling my promise made me feel closer to her. My grandparents died several years ago, and my mother was an only child, like me. And there's no one else in my family. So she was worried. Poor little Sophie, all alone in the world. She thought maybe Malcolm could at least offer me fellowship and family."

"So you're sure that it's him? There's no doubt in your mind?"

"I don't think Mom would have led me astray about something like that on her deathbed," Sophie said. "But I still tested Ava's DNA. I swiped a champagne glass at the reception announcing their engagement. She's definitely my cousin. This trip to San Francisco was my first chance to get close enough to Malcolm to get a sample from him."

"And did you?"

She gave him a sheepish smile. "I did, actually. The other night, when you found me in his office? I was in the bathroom, stealing his water glass. I'd already swiped his dessert fork. They're wrapped up in bubble wrap, packed in my suitcase. So if it looked like I was sneaking around in there, I guess I was. Stealing flatware and glassware."

"Wow," he murmured.

"I needed hard objective proof," she explained. "I didn't want to have to defend my mom's truthfulness, of my own. So I'm covering all my bases. But truthfully? I don't know if I can stand to wait any longer. It took almost four weeks to get results that last time, for Ava's DNA."

"No, don't wait any longer," Vann said. "Just do it."

"I've been taking my time, just watching them," Sophie said. "Some families are poisonous. But from the looks of this wedding, the Maddoxes aren't."

"No, they are not," Vann said. "They're solid. Not perfect, but solid."

Sophie crossed her arms over her chest. She felt vulnerable…but hopeful. "You know these people well. So you don't think they'd ride me out of town on a rail if I come forward with this?"

"By no means," he said. "I think you'd be a great addition to their family. You'd fit right in. You're smart, tough, talented, accomplished, gorgeous. You'd just be another jewel in their crown."

"Oh, please," she scoffed.

"It's the objective truth," Vann said. "As far as looks are concerned, they've got great genes going for them, and you are no exception to that rule."

Sophie walked out of the bathroom, sat down on the bed and unbuckled the ankle strap on her sandal. "I know that Malcolm raised Ava and Drew after their parents were killed," she said. "I was afraid that if I came out of nowhere and claimed to be Malcolm's daughter, they might get jealous and possessive. Protective, even. He's like their dad, in every way that counts. I'd understand if they did."

Vann shrugged. "Who can say how they'll feel? People are complicated. But they'll get over it because they're not stupid or spiteful. And they'll do the right thing because that's who they are. In the end, they'll be glad they did."

Sophie was so relieved at Vann's reaction her eyes were fogging again. She wiped away the tears, laughing. "Wow. That's an extremely positive spin on this whole situation."

"That's how I see it," he said. "Drew's my best friend. I trust him. I respect Malcolm. I don't know Ava as well, but I like her, and Drew worships his baby sister. I know you. You're amazing. What's not to be positive about? It's a win/win for everyone."

"That's sweet, Vann, but it would be silly to think there's no downside."

"I don't see it," he said. "Having you in their lives is like finding buried treasure."

"Aww! Don't go overboard," she warned him. "I'm already overwhelmed from the party. Thinking about how it might have been if Mom had been a part of the Maddox family. And me, for that matter. I could have been one of them. It just got to me somehow. All the lost chances. Brothers or sisters I might have had. It's silly, I know."

"It's not silly at all." Vann sat down on the bed and clasped her hand.

"I know that the past is gone," she said. "The mistakes are over and done with. There's no point in thinking about them."

"Except to learn from them," he said. "To not repeat them."

She gave him a wry look. "I'm not having an affair with a married man, Vann. Nor will I find myself with a surprise pregnancy."

"Actually, I was thinking about my own father," he said. "He never let down his guard. Not with my mom and not with me. It was probably his PTSD, but it marked him forever. Maybe it was that way for your mom, too. And Malcolm."

Sophie nodded. "Mom never let down her guard, either," she said quietly. "She had the occasional date now and again, but she couldn't let herself care that much about anyone again. Except for me."

"That won't be us." Vann pressed his lips to her hand.

Sophie let out a shaky laugh. "It's so strange," she said. "But I just can't keep up my guard with you. No matter how I try."

Vann shook his head, gazing into her eyes. "So don't try."

The moment was so fragile. Delicate. A rainbow-tinted bubble, made of longing and possibility. With feelings so powerful she could barely stand their charge.

They made her shake with fear. And hope.

She stroked Vann's face, memorizing every tiny detail. He moved her, excited her. So beautiful, with those serious dark eyes.

He reached out slowly to unfasten her dress, working loose the hook she'd sewn under the fabric rose. He opened it and pushed the light, sheer wrap off.

Sophie tossed her hair back, but couldn't help a self-conscious glance down at the frilly neckline of the under-dress, dipping low to show the entire length of the scar on her chest. Her hand drifted up to cover it.

Vann's hand covered it first. Her heart felt like it was thudding against her ribs.

"Beautiful," he whispered.

"What?" she asked.

"Your heart," he said. "It's been through so much, but it's so strong."

She smiled at him. "It's galloping like a racehorse." She tugged the soft fabric of her bodice, peeling it down over her breasts, freeing her arms.

"Mine, too," he said hoarsely. He slid his hands down from her shoulders to cup her breasts.

Her hunger was too urgent to put up with teasing games. She reached back and unhooked the bra, tossing it aside.

He got up and stripped off his tux, tossing item after item in the general direction of the chair. Some hit, some missed. He didn't seem to care. Sophie pushed the covers down and then took off her dress and panties. Soon he was pressing her into the sheets.

Oh, *yes*. The heat of his big body was a shock to her system. He tasted so good. Like whiskey and coffee. Hot and wet. She gasped with pleasure as he situated himself over her. The length of his hot, stiff shaft rested against her most sensitive folds without entering her. Just slowly caressing her. Sliding and teasing. Driving her mad as he ravaged her mouth with those frantic kisses.

Sophie moved against him, sensually at first, but it soon turned to moaning desperation, fighting to get him where she needed him—deep inside her.

"Take it easy," he murmured. "The longer you wait, the better it will be."

She laughed with what breath she could. "Please don't tease."

"Not tonight." Vann shifted his weight, nudging himself inside her.

They sighed in agonized delight as he slowly pushed inside. Every moment of it was an exquisite, shuddering bliss. Every part of her so sensitive, alive to sensation. As if she were being painted with light, and every stroke made her glow brighter.

Every deep, surging stroke made her crazy for the

next one. A frenzy of need. An explosion of bliss. She lost herself in it.

As she came back to earth, she was afraid to open her eyes. That it would be like the night before. She'd be floating on air, and he would have those grim shadows in his eyes.

But he didn't. He was smiling.

"Hey," he said. "There you are at last. I was about to send out a search party."

She felt almost weak with relief. "I was destroyed. Beautifully destroyed."

"Same." He stroked his hand slowly over her hip. "Incredible."

"So, ah…what's different tonight?"

His hands stopped. "Meaning?"

"For you," she specified. "Yesterday the sex was amazing, but you weren't happy. What changed for you?"

His grin dug gorgeous, sexy grooves into his cheeks. "Maybe I'm letting my guard down, too."

"You seem relieved," she said.

A puzzled line formed between his brows. "In what way?"

"I think I scared you, asking you to keep my deep dark secret," she said. "What on earth where you afraid I was going to say?"

"In my experience, long-kept secrets usually aren't happy things," Vann said. "Otherwise, why would they be secret?"

"Like our hot affair?" She batted her eyes at him teasingly.

"I can't keep that a secret anymore," he said. "I'm sorry, but I just can't."

She gave him a stern look. “You will not add to my burden right now.”

“But I want to stay here all night,” he said. “I want to walk out with you in the morning and go to breakfast. Brazenly. Holding hands.”

“In your tux?” she teased. “You naughty boy.”

He laughed. “Fine, so I’ll get a change of clothes. But that’s not the point. I want to sit with you at the breakfast table. Pour your champagne. Peel your grapes.”

She laughed at him. “Whoa! Serious stuff!”

“Remember what you said on the beach? When I asked what it would take to be able to hold your hand?”

“I remember,” she said.

“I’m ready,” he said. “I want to do the work. Whatever needs to be done so I have the right to hold your hand on the beach, or hover over you at the breakfast buffet, or be stuck to you, any damn place we want.”

“Slow down,” she said gently.

“Why?” he demanded. “Why waste time? I want to show you off. You’re a prize. I want to flaunt you to the world. I can’t play it cool. I want to court you.”

“I like being courted,” she said, her hand trailing down over his belly until it reached his erection. “I suggest that you start by demonstrating exactly what I stand to gain from your offer.”

“You got it,” he said as he covered her mouth with his.

Sixteen

"Noon would be fine," Vann told the employee at the car rental employee. He finished his business, closed the call and pushed the bathroom door open.

Sophie was awake and smiling at him. Morning sunlight spilled through the lofted skylight. The light showed the deep red highlights in her glossy brown hair. She stretched luxuriously, and the movement made the sheet twist and tighten around her gorgeous body. "Who are you talking to?" she asked.

"Sorry I woke you," he said.

She saw the clock and jerked up with a gasp. "Oh, God. The limo! We're so late!"

"No, we're not," Vann said.

"It's supposed to leave in fifteen minutes, and I'm not even packed!"

"You don't have to take the limo," he told her. "I just

rented a car. A convertible. I got online this morning, while you were still asleep. They're driving it over for me. I figured, no one expects us at work today, and the weather's holding, so maybe we could spend the day exploring the coast together. We can make our way back to Seattle this evening." He paused, and added delicately, "Or not. If you're in a hurry to get back."

A belated smile broke out all over her face. "That sounds like a blast."

"Great," he said. "They're dropping it off at noon. That gives us time for breakfast."

"Time for the walk of shame, eh?" she teased. "Back to change the tux?"

"I'll live," he said, but flushed as memories of last night's erotic play flashed through his mind.

"Well, then." She stretched, letting the sheet drop to her waist. "Why don't you go get dressed and get your suitcase ready, and I'll do the same. Then come on back, and we'll go in to breakfast together."

He grinned as he buttoned his shirt. "Do I get to hold your hand as we go in?"

She tilted her head to the side, considering her answer carefully. "If you like," she conceded. "But you're not peeling my grapes. A girl's got to draw the line somewhere."

"No grapes," he agreed swiftly.

She got up, sauntered over to him naked and kissed him.

"You're making it hard for me to leave," he murmured, his voice thick.

"Your problem," she whispered. "Not mine."

He seized her. "Aw, hell. The walk of shame can wait."

* * *

The breakfast crowd had thinned out by the time they finally got to the dining room. Many of the wedding guests had left already but there were more than enough people still there to notice the grand entrance. Holding hands, at Vann's insistence. It made her face hot, but it was a symbolic thing. A milestone.

Drew and Jenna noticed immediately. Drew grinned, Jenna looked delighted and Ava fluttered her fingers and winked. Even Bev, sitting with Hendrick in the corner, blew Sophie a benevolent kiss.

Tim Bryce was there, with Rich. Both men gave her a cold stare. She wasn't too surprised. She'd been curt with Rich the day before. She didn't regret it.

"It looks like Malcolm's gone back," she said. "He must have caught the limo. I was going to ask if I could schedule a meeting for tomorrow. I'm going to take your advice, and meet with him now. The testing can wait. If he needs proof."

"There's Sylvia, having breakfast," Vann said. "Have her set up a meeting. He would have told you to talk to her, anyway. Let's ask her right now."

Wow, this was all getting very real, very fast. She felt rushed, but there was no reason she could think of to put it off, so they walked over to Sylvia's table.

Sylvia's eyes had a speculative twinkle over the rim of her coffee cup as they approached.

"Good morning, Vann," she said. "Looks like you've been busy."

"Always am, Syl. Sophie needs to schedule a meeting with Malcolm as soon as possible," Vann said. "Will he be in the office tomorrow?"

Sylvia pulled a tablet out of her bag, opened a scheduling app and flicked through it. "You're in luck," she said. "Usually he doesn't come in on Tuesdays, but he's playing catch-up after the wedding and San Francisco. I could put you in for ten thirty."

"That's great," Sophie said faintly.

"Done." Sylvia tapped the keypad with a stylus. "See you tomorrow."

They seated themselves near the window. Vann studied Sophie's face as they waited for the waiter to bring coffee. "You look nervous," he observed. "Don't be."

"It just hit me," she said. "I wasn't expecting things to move this fast. The documentation phase was easier. Guess I'm more chicken than I knew. I almost regret not waiting for another test."

"Do you want me to be there tomorrow?" he offered.

Sophie smiled at him. "Thanks, but this should be just between me and him."

"In any case, let's meet for lunch after," Vann said. "That way you can debrief me."

Sophie gladly agreed to that. Their eggs Benedict arrived, and they took their time with their breakfast before getting on their way.

The day that followed was perfect in every way. Not just because of the sexy little car, the beautiful weather, the stunning scenery.

It was the way she felt. The melting warmth all through her body. The company of this man made her tingle and glow and laugh constantly. They had long, winding conversations about everything that popped into their minds. There were no awkward pauses. Even the pauses seemed right and natural, full of their own proper significance.

The sky was cloudy, but there was no rain, just stunning moments when sun burst through the clouds, illuminating the sea. They stopped at every scenic vantage point, strolled barefoot on every beach. When they got hungry, they picked up some fish and chips and cold beers at a boardwalk restaurant and ate on the sand on a beach blanket that Vann had bought at the first tourist shop they came across.

That was followed by double-decker ice-cream cones, and a lively difference of opinion about the relative merits of milk chocolate versus dark chocolate. The dispute was never resolved, but the argument required multiple taste tests, which soon turned into chilled, chocolatey kisses. After a few minutes of that, someone drove past them and yelled, "Get a room!"

Vann pulled away with some difficulty. "We could," he murmured.

"Get a room, you mean?"

"In a heartbeat," he said.

"I'd love it," she said. "But tomorrow is a big day for me, and I don't want to get back to the city late."

"I guess we should hit the road, then. As it is, we'll reach Seattle after dark."

"I hate to go," she said. "Hey, watch out. Ice cream is dripping on your shoes."

They set out again. With the top down, it was too noisy for conversation, but Vann held her hand whenever he didn't need it on the gearshift or the wheel. The feeling that hummed between them transcended words.

The occasional glance or smile was enough. No barriers.

Vann turned to her when they got close to the city.

"I'll take you home if you want," he said. "But my house is close. On Lake Washington."

She hesitated, thinking about tomorrow's meeting. But being with Vann made her feel brave and fearless, and naturally lovable. She could use every last drop of that feeling. It would give her courage. "I have one last outfit in my bag that would be acceptable in a work setting," she said.

"Do you need to get any lab documentation from home?" he asked. "Like the test on Ava's DNA?"

"I have the documents on my computer at home, but I also have them on my tablet, right here in my bag," she told him. "I'm all set for this meeting."

"So you'll stay with me? Can I take you home?"

After a single suspended breath, she smiled at him.

"Yes," she said softly. "Take me home."

Seventeen

Vann's house didn't seem big from the road that circled the lake, but on the other side, it opened up and revealed itself to be larger than it seemed, with a terrace looking out over the water. The entrance led to the upper floor, and corridors led to bedrooms on either side. Then a wide, shallow staircase in the foyer under a big skylight led down to a huge central space that opened off into a dining room, living room and kitchen, all with spectacular walls of glass to showcase the view.

"What a beautiful place," Sophie murmured.

"I can't take credit for it," he said. "Drew designed it. I told him in broad strokes what I wanted, and he made it happen. Better than my wildest dreams. One of the perks of having a best buddy who's a world-class architect."

He hung up her coat and turned the lights on in the

kitchen. "I'm too distracted to cook," he said. "But I've got some take-out favorites I can recommend. A Thai place, a Japanese place, a Middle Eastern restaurant, Indian. And some really excellent Italian."

"I'm fussy about Italian, since it's my heritage," she teased. "Excellent?"

"You won't know until you try," he said.

"Then I opt for the Italian," she said.

Vann picked out a menu from the bundle in his drawer. "Want to take a look?"

"You know their dishes," she said. "You pick this time."

He grabbed his smartphone and dialed as he uncorked a bottle of red wine. "Hello?...Yes, this is Vann Acosta. I'd like an order delivered to the usual address. Let's start with the smoked salmon. Fresh artichoke salad, stuffed mushroom, batter-fried spring vegetables, the half-moon smoked cheese ravioli with butter and sage. Fresh greens with orange and fennel. Grilled cacciatore sausage. Panna cotta with blackberry topping for dessert. All of this is for two...Excellent...Yes. Put it on the usual card."

Sophie gave him a shocked look. "That's a lot of food. Overdoing it much?"

He poured the wine. His hungry, lingering glance made her nipples tighten. "I'm burning off the calories just looking at you." He held out the glass. "Come on back to the lake."

She followed him out into the water-scented air on the terrace, listening in the stillness for the hollow sound of water slapping the pebbles on the beach. City lights gleamed on the dark ripples. Wind ruffled the water's surface like a stroking hand.

"It's beautiful," she murmured. "So peaceful."

"I was actually the first one to buy waterfront property here," he said. "Then Drew decided he liked the lake, too, and he found another piece of land. So he's my neighbor, just mile or so up that way." He pointed.

"How wonderful, to have a friend nearby. Do you guys hang out on weekends?"

He snorted. "What weekends? We see each other mostly at work. At least until he met Jenna, at which point I basically stopped seeing him at all. Not that I begrudge him his happiness." Vann smiled at her. "Now less than ever."

Sophie raised her glass. "To Drew and Jenna. May their love endure forever."

"To Drew and Jenna," Vann echoed.

They clinked glasses, and drank. He reached out to stroke the side of her cheek with his knuckle. "So soft," he said. "It's amazing how soft your skin is."

"Usually I feel as hard as glass," she said. "You make me feel soft."

He reached down to grab her hand. "We have to stay close enough to the house to hear the doorbell," he told her. "They usually don't make me wait very long for the food."

They'd only just finished their first glass of wine when the delivery arrived. Vann brought in the food and set the table, dragging out some candles and candleholders.

They spread the containers out, and feasted by candlelight.

At a certain point, the conversation wound down into long, speaking silences. They gazed at each other, feeling the sweet, delicious anticipation build.

This looked and felt so…well…real. This fantasy of happiness, pleasure and love. It felt like a future. A family. Something she'd never quite been able to envision for herself.

Against all odds, this actually seemed to be real.

Vann stood up and held out his hand. "Are you ready to go upstairs?"

She got up and took his hand. "Lead the way," she said.

The night was a feverish erotic fantasy. After the first few wild, frenzied times they made love, they slowed down, dozing from time to time, tightly twined together.

Vann was too happy to sleep. He just stroked Sophie's hair, his throat too tight to speak, his chest bursting with emotion. He craved more of her. Now and forever.

Dawn was lightening the sky outside. Tendrils of mist rose off the lake, creating an ethereal, otherworldly realm where nothing could intrude on their love. They gazed at each other until gazing wasn't enough, and it turned to kissing, tasting, stroking. She caressed him boldly, guiding him into her tight, slick warmth. They rocked together in a surging dance of pleasure that crested into yet another explosion of delight.

They lay together afterward, lost in each other's eyes. Sophie's hands moving over his chest, fingertips sliding through the hair that arrowed down from his chest to his belly.

"It's such a strange feeling," she said.

"Which one?" he asked. "I'm fielding a lot of them."

"Being so open," she admitted. "I let my guard down so far, I don't even know where I left it."

"Me, too," he admitted.

"Does it feel good?" she asked hesitantly.

"Great," he assured her. "Let's never put our guard back up. Not with each other."

Sophie put his hand to her lips, kissing his knuckles. "It's a deal," she whispered.

He felt like his heart was too big for his chest as the meaning of her whispered words sank in. They were taking a step into something so rare and pure and precious. He was humbled, dazzled to realize it. She trusted him. It was such a gift.

He wanted to be a better man. To fully deserve that trust.

"What time is it?" she asked.

"Really early," he said. "But I'm too jacked up to sleep any longer. It's a big day. I'll make you a good breakfast."

He bounded out of bed, threw on a pair of sweatpants and went down to get to work.

The dining room was a mess from last night's feast, but the breakfast nook was still pristine, so he set up there. By the time Sophie came down, swathed in his blue terry-cloth bathrobe, her hair a mass of damp waves, he had breakfast sausages, English muffins, OJ and coffee on the table, and was tipping a panful of eggs, two for her, four for him, onto the plates. He hadn't felt this hungry since he was a teenager.

"Wow," she said, impressed. "Look at you, pampering me. Don't tell anyone."

He poured her coffee. "I don't care who sees me," he said. "I'll do it out in front of God and everyone."

"Whew." She sank into her chair and sipped her coffee, smiling. "Scandal."

"Bring it on," he said. "I'm so wound up. I'll try to chill."

"No, don't. I like you like this. It excites me."

Their eyes locked. The air ignited.

Sophie looked away first, laughing. "Not now, for God's sake! There's no time!"

"Soon," he promised. "I'll pamper you again. Until you can't even see straight."

"Mmm, something to look forward to."

He realized, over halfway through the meal, that having breakfast with a lover was a first for him. He never stayed with anyone all through the night. Never wanted to.

But everything about Sophie was different. New.

After breakfast they got dressed. Sophie was as stunning as ever when she was all put together, in a silver-gray linen tunic over matching wide-legged trousers and gray suede pumps. Her hair was loose, styled in long waves and curls. Her lips were a glossy red, and her whiskey-colored eyes were full of mystery as she looked him over. "Nice suit," she said. "I think we're both presentable."

"Should we take the convertible to go to work?"

"I wish." She shook her head with a regretful smile. "I'd ruin my hair. Not today."

"No problem," he assured her. "We can take my Jag."

Morning traffic was what it always was in Seattle, but he was too euphoric to be frustrated today. It meant more time with Sophie. And as early as they'd risen, they got there with time to spare.

"Can you let me out at the front entrance?" Sophie asked as they got closer to the downtown office. "I need to take care of some things before the rest of the staff gets in."

He pulled over in front of the building. "I'll be at your office at 12:15."

She had a shadow of lingering doubt on her face. "Shouldn't we just meet at the restaurant? For now, anyway?"

He shook his head, resolute. "We're through with that now. Onward."

She gave him a smile that made his body tingle. "You are just on fire today, Vann."

"You lit the flame," he said.

Her laughter sounded happy. "Okay, fine. My office, then. Later."

"Good luck with the meeting," he called. "I know it'll be fine. He's a lucky man."

Her smile left him just staring helplessly after her until the cars started beeping impatiently behind him.

Vann floated through the morning in a haze. Then Zack leaned inside his office.

"Hey," he said. "Do you have a quick debrief for me before I go to Malcolm's office?"

Vann looked at him blankly. "Debrief about what?"

Zack frowned. "Your info-gathering project? Sophie Valente? The IP theft?"

"Oh, that. I'll give you the short version. Not her. Look elsewhere."

Zack's face froze. Then he stepped inside and closed the door behind him. "You're sure of this?" he said. "You have proof?"

"You need to prove guilt, not innocence," Vann said. "I know her now."

"What, in the biblical sense?"

Vann stood up. "What the hell is that supposed to mean?"

"Sorry," Zack said. "I guess that wasn't appropriate."

"No, it wasn't," Vann said through his teeth. "What I meant was, I know exactly what Sophie Valente is after here at Maddox Hill. And it's not money."

"So what is it?"

Vann hesitated. "I'll leave that for her to reveal. It's not my place to tell."

"She'd better hurry up about it," Zack said. "And she better be prepared to defend herself. From what I heard Bryce say, he's got her in the bag."

A chill seized him. "Bryce is full of shit."

"I won't say you're wrong, but if he has the ironclad proof he says he has, Sophie's in trouble."

"Bryce can't have proof," Vann said. "He's going down a dead end."

"Be that as it may, he's meeting with Malcolm now," Zack told him. "Explaining his discoveries."

"But Sophie was supposed to meet with him. In just a few minutes, in fact. We were supposed to talk with Malcolm and Bryce about all this tomorrow."

"Malcolm got in early," Zack said. "I heard him complaining about Sylvia scheduling back-to-back meetings this morning. Evidently Bryce couldn't wait until tomorrow. He looked buzzed. I was just going there, but I wanted to check in with you first."

"He can't be showing Malcolm what he discovered,"

Vann repeated. "There's nothing to discover! I'll go and tell Malcolm myself."

"Steady, now," Zack cautioned. "You're not currently in the best position to come to Sophie Valente's defense. Keep that in mind."

"Because I'm in love with her, you mean?" Vann said. "I'm not ashamed of it."

Zack winced. "This is worse than I thought."

Vann was already out the door. Zack caught up and kept pace with him as he made his way to Malcolm's office. Sylvia gave him a disapproving look as he approached.

"I'm going in to see Malcolm," he said.

"And a pleasant good morning to you, too, Vann. I'm sorry, but you can't quite go in yet! Tim Bryce is in there with him. Vann…hey! Vann, he's in a meeting!"

Malcolm's office door flew open. Malcolm poked his head out. "Sylvia!" he bawled. "Get Zack and Vann in here right—oh, there you are. Get your butts in here this instant."

Vann and Zack filed past Sylvia. She leaned in the door. "Do you gentlemen need coffee or—"

"They can drink coffee on their own damn time," Malcolm snarled. "Leave us."

Sylvia quickly closed the door. Malcolm's face was splotchy with anger as he rounded on them. "You two have been keeping secrets from me, eh?"

"No, we haven't," Zack said evenly. "We've been taking care of business, just like we always do."

Malcolm gestured at Vann. "I've seen some of his business lately. I'm not impressed."

"You've got it wrong, Malcolm," Vann said.

"No, he doesn't," Bryce said. "On the contrary, I

think he's nailed it. Quite literally." Bryce chortled at his own joke, but the snickering died out as Vann fixed his icy gaze on him. "It's her," he said, his voice triumphant. "What I just showed Malcolm is airtight."

Vann breathed down the urge to punch that smug, self-satisfied look right off Bryce's smirking face. "What do you think you've got on her?"

"I don't think it, I know it. Look for yourself. I have a video of Sophie Valente stealing documents out of Malcolm's laptop."

"That's impossible," Vann said.

"It's a fact," Malcolm said heavily. "I saw it. The video is time-stamped. She's in the dress she wore at the wedding. I recognize my hotel room. There's no mistaking her. To think I invited a lying thief to my own nephew's wedding and let her mix with all the people I care most about. And the sensitive information she heard in the Zhang Wei meetings, God help us."

"I thought Vann's plan was to get more information before we went any further with our investigation." Bryce's voice was oily with insinuation. "Looks like he took the job more literally than we ever dreamed."

Zack blew out a sharp breath. "I want to see that video, right now."

They circled the desk and gathered around the monitor. Bryce edged closer but kept the length of the desk between himself and Vann. "I rigged cameras on the walkway leading to your room at Paradise Point," Bryce began.

"I doubt that's legal," Zack said. "Privacy laws—"

"Shut up and watch," Malcolm said. "Show them the clip from the walkway."

Bryce tapped the mouse and set the video clip to

play. The camera was trained on one of the wooden walkways at Paradise Point, the rhododendron branches swaying gently and casting shadows on the weathered planks.

Sophie appeared, walking briskly and purposefully. She paused, frowning, and lifted her arm to check the time on her glittering gold wristwatch. She moved swiftly out of the camera's frame.

"You will all agree that's Sophie Valente. Correct?" Bryce said.

Vann ignored the question. "What time was it?"

"The video clock shows that it was 3:51," Bryce replied. "The ceremony began less than ten minutes later. She picked her time carefully. Everyone was already assembled on the lawn for the wedding. Now look at this." He fast-forwarded until there was another flash of pink, then ran the video back and set it to Play.

It was Sophie again, coming back the other way. Still frowning. The wind tossed her hair over her face. This time, she was almost running.

"Four minutes and twenty-five seconds," Bryce said. "Just a couple of minutes after that, Rich saw her in the entrance hall and told her she was late for the ceremony. The two of them came in together, as I'm sure you noticed."

Vann looked into Bryce's face, his gaze unwavering. "Sophie told me that a woman who claimed to be on the resort staff told her to go to Malcolm's suite right before the wedding was scheduled to begin."

Malcolm made a derisive sound. "My suite? Right before the ceremony? What for? That's absurd!"

"She thought so, too," Vann said. "This mystery person told her that you were there and that you needed her to interpret something. Obviously, she found no one in the room. She said she knocked, waited for a couple of minutes—"

"Four minutes and twenty-five seconds, to be exact," Bryce said. "That's how long she was inside his suite."

"She never went inside," Vann said. "She and I discussed it. And they told her at the front desk that the woman who sent her to Malcolm's room had never worked there."

"Well now," Malcolm said. "Isn't that convenient."

"Are you interested in seeing what happened in Malcolm's room during that interval, or not?" Bryce asked.

"For God's sake, Tim, just play the damn thing," Malcolm growled. "Gloating is in poor taste, and I'm not in the mood."

Bryce tapped on the keyboard for a moment. "I'm emailing a courtesy copy of these clips to both of you," he said. "Review them at your leisure." He shot a sly glance at Vann. "Something to remember her by?"

"Tim!" Malcolm barked. "What did I just say?"

"Sorry." Bryce hit Play and stepped back. "Enjoy."

The video was shot from the wall behind the desk. The room was dimly lit. At 4:34, they saw a dark silhouette position herself on the desk chair in front of the open laptop.

The figure reached out to hit the mouse, and the computer came to life, flooding the figure in the chair with cool blue light.

It was Sophie, in that same silk chiffon thing she'd worn at the wedding. She stared into the screen, seeming serene and absorbed, typed rapidly for a moment and then lifted her phone, as she'd done in the video Bryce had shown them the previous week, before the

San Francisco trip. She was taking pictures of the screen.

"I loaded the laptop with dummy files," Bryce said. "Just for her. They look very convincing, but all the details and calculations have been scrambled. Her buyer is going to be very angry. I'm afraid our bad little girl is in for quite a spanking."

"Don't talk about her that way," Vann growled.

"Not another word out of you," Malcolm said. "You're in no position to criticize."

The video continued. Just Sophie looking calmly into the screen. She would lift the phone, focus, snap the picture. Lift, focus, snap. Her long hair hung over her shoulders, the waves and curls smoothly arranged.

At a certain point, she dropped her phone into her beaded bag and put the computer to sleep. A blurry shifting of shadows in the dark, a brightening as she opened the door to leave—and it was over.

Vann felt rooted to the ground. His brain seemed frozen. It wouldn't process this information. The woman he knew, the woman he was in love with—she could not have done this. It just...wasn't...possible.

"Well?" Bryce said. "Does that satisfy you?"

"*Satisfy* is not the word I'd use," Malcolm said slowly. "But it's certainly damning evidence. I don't think I need anything more to be convinced of her guilt. Not much more to say about it, eh, Vann?"

"You have to let her defend herself," Vann said. "She may have an explanation. Something we don't know about. Something we've overlooked."

"What explanation can she have for being inside my private room?" Malcolm demanded. "Now that I think about it, she turned up in my guest office in the

San Francisco meeting, too. Remember? That's where I found the two of you, as I recall. Did she go in before you went in, Vann?"

Vann had to force himself to speak. "Yes. A couple of minutes before me. I saw her heading in there, and chased after her to see if she was up to anything. She wasn't."

"So she hadn't told you to meet her there," Malcolm persisted.

"No," Vann admitted reluctantly. "I surprised her."

"And she distracted you by coming on to you," Bryce said, smirking. "Well, that's a classic move. Nothing like sex to distract a man. I hardly blame you. Except that I do."

"Shut up, Tim," Malcolm said. "There is nothing amusing about this situation. So she might have been snooping around on my computer in there, too."

"No," Vann said. "She didn't go near your computer. She was in the bathroom."

"Really?" Malcolm grunted. "Public ladies' room not good enough for her, then?"

Vann didn't answer. His face felt numb.

"Well, Vann?" Malcolm said. "You've got your work cut out for you."

Vann looked at him, baffled. "Come again? What work?"

"You're the one who has to do it," Malcolm went on. "You know her best."

"Do what?"

Malcolm made an impatient sound. "Stop playing dumb. Get her to come clean about everything she's done up to now. Every detail, every dollar. Do it, if you care about her at all. Persuade her to cooperate. I'll be as lenient as I possibly can if she does."

His mouth was bone-dry. He forced out a rasping croak. "I can't."

"It has to be you," Malcolm said. "Would you rather she spend the best years of her life in jail? Don't make me be the bad guy here, Vann. Help me out. Help her out."

The intercom buzzed. "Mr. Maddox?" Sylvia said. "Ms. Valente is here for your ten-thirty meeting. Shall I have her wait until you gentlemen have finished, or shall I reschedule her for later on?"

"No, Sylvia, send her on in," Malcolm said.

"Are you sure?" Sylvia sounded baffled. "With everyone still there?"

"Exactly." Malcolm glared around at each of them. "Why drag this out?"

The worst-case scenario was unfolding before Vann's eyes with terrifying speed. His belly clenched with dread. Then the door opened and Sophie walked in.

Suddenly, all at once, Vann remembered the powerful rationale he'd always instinctively understood for keeping up one's guard. Love had made him forget that basic, elemental rule of nature.

You kept up your guard to not get annihilated.

Eighteen

Sophie stopped the minute she entered Malcolm's office, startled to see so many people there. Including Vann.

He didn't smile. In fact, his face was a blank, tight mask. It reminded her of something sad, something painful. It came to her after a split second.

Mom's face, that last, terrible week before she died. It was the bloodless tension in a person's expression when they were trying not to show intense pain. She almost asked Vann if he was okay, but then Malcolm spoke.

"Good morning, Ms. Valente."

She turned back to Malcolm, who was behind his desk with Zack Austin and Tim Bryce, of all people. "Sorry to interrupt," she said. "I can find a better time if—"

"Not at all," Malcolm said. "Go on. Say whatever you need to say."

Sophie was taken aback. Something was off, and she was smack-dab in the middle of it, with no clue. "Are you sure—"

"I am. Please, just say it, whatever it is. Out with it."

Oh-kayyyy…fine. She took a careful, calming breath. "Actually, what I wanted to discuss with you is of a private nature. I'd prefer to speak with you alone."

Malcolm studied her from under heavy, furrowed eyebrows. "I think not," he said. "Anything you have to say can certainly be said in front of these people."

This was all wrong, and it gave her chills. But it wasn't like she could retreat in confusion. That would look mealy-mouthed and cowardly and just…well, weird. As if she were somehow in the wrong. Trying to hide something, trying to pull something.

What the hell. She'd do this for Mom. If this bombed, she'd just leave this place forever and start fresh elsewhere. She gave Vann another swift glance, hoping for a smile, a signal. Any sign of solidarity.

He wasn't even looking at her. It was starting to scare her.

"I came in to see you because I have something important and very personal to tell you," she said. "It involves us both."

"Tell it," Malcolm said. But he did not beckon for her to move closer to his desk, nor did he offer her a chair.

Tim grabbed a chair and sat down, looking at her like she was the main attraction. What on earth?

"Bryce," Zack said under his breath. "Do not start."

"I didn't say a word," Tim said. "Don't mind me. I'm just watching the show."

That pissed her off too much to keep silent. "I didn't come in here to put on a show for you, Tim."

"I guess that remains to be seen, hmm?"

Sophie turned her attention from him and approached Malcolm's desk despite his marked lack of an invitation. She'd be damned if she was going to cower by the door, ready to bolt like a scared little bunny.

She squared her shoulders. "I asked for this meeting because I have decided to tell you that I am your biological daughter," she announced.

Malcolm's face was absolutely blank as seconds of painful silence ticked by.

She wanted to break the silence, but it was his place to make the next move. Tim's mouth hung open. Zack looked startled. The only one who didn't look shocked was Vann—but he still looked like he was hiding mortal agony behind a mask.

She looked back at Malcolm. His eyes were downcast now.

"I see. So… Vicky," he said hoarsely. He coughed to clear his throat. "You're Vicky Valente's daughter, correct? You look like her. I noticed your surname when you were introduced. It's not an uncommon name, so I never dreamed you might be related to her."

And to you. "So you remember her?"

He put his hand up to his eyes. "Of course I remember Vicky. How is she?"

"She died, not long ago," Sophie said. "April of last year. Pancreatic cancer."

Malcolm covered his eyes again. Almost a minute went by before he cleared his throat with a sharp cough.

"I'm very sorry to hear that," he said. "You have my sincere condolences."

"Thank you," Sophie said, bemused. And then she just stood there, in the awkward silence. Waiting.

This was so weird. The hard part was done. He hadn't thrown her out, or yelled at her, or laughed in her face, or called her a liar. He hadn't denied ever knowing her mother. Those were the outcomes she had feared, and none of them had come to pass.

So why did the air still feel so thick in here? And why did Vann and Zack look like they were being forced to witness an execution?

Tim, on the other hand, looked like he should be munching buttered popcorn.

"So you believe my claim?" she asked. "I was born in New York City, nine months after you and she worked together on the Phelps Pavilion."

"I do not disbelieve it." Malcolm's voice was expressionless.

Sophie pulled her tablet out of her bag, opening the files. "This is my birth certificate. I got a sample of Ava's DNA several weeks ago. I had it analyzed by a local genetics lab, and these are the results. As you can see, there's an overwhelming probability that she's my close relative. At least a cousin."

"I see." Malcolm didn't even lean forward to look at the birth certificate or the genetics lab test results. Which was not promising.

"I also took the opportunity to get a sample of your DNA when we were in San Francisco," she said. "Not because of any doubts I had, since I believe what Mom told me, but just because I wanted objective proof, for your sake. I took a fork and a water glass from your office in San Francisco. But then I decided I couldn't wait to have the results analyzed to speak to you. The stress of keeping this secret was getting to me."

"This explains a lot," Tim said.

"Your contribution was not requested, Tim," Malcolm said.

Tim made a lip-zipping gesture. Sophie looked around at all the men present in the room and threw up her hands. "This explains what?" she demanded.

But no one answered. "Come on, people!" she said. "What the hell is going on in here? What aren't you telling me?"

"One thing at a time," Malcolm said. "Why didn't you tell me immediately? You've been working here for months. Why not come to me before?"

"I wanted to line up objective, scientific proof," Sophie said. "Plus, I had to work up the nerve. I couldn't just pop out of nowhere with an announcement like that."

"I see," he said. "And what exactly did you hope to gain from this revelation?"

Sophie flinched inwardly. It wasn't a surprise, of course, but it still hurt, that he would automatically assume that her motives were just money-grubbing avarice.

"Nothing financial, if that's what you're wondering," she said. "I have many hard-won and highly marketable professional skills. I could make an excellent living anywhere in the world that I chose to go. I also have inherited a considerable amount of money and property from my mother's side of the family. I own homes in Singapore, New York City, the Catskills, Florence and Positano. I don't need one penny from you. I wouldn't even need to work, strictly speaking, but I wasn't cut out to be a bored socialite. I need challenge in my life."

Malcolm cleared his throat. "It's a lot to take in all at once. So if you are independently wealthy as you say, then what do want from me, Ms. Valente?"

Damn. It was a bad sign if he had to ask.

"Please, call me Sophie," she said stiffly. "My mother asked me to come to you. It was a deathbed request. She wanted us to know each other. She was worried about the fact that I have no living family left. It's mostly for her sake that I'm here. I promised her I'd come and tell you about myself."

She and Malcolm stared at each other. Her heart sank. Malcolm didn't look angry, or defensive, or even suspicious. Just sad.

"I would be satisfied just to be known to you," she said hesitantly. "And acknowledged by you. I would be open to us getting to know each other as people, if that interests you. I've enjoyed my time working here, and I've done my best for the company. I'd also like to get acquainted with my cousins. Ava and Drew seem well worth knowing."

"That they are," he said.

Sophie tapped on the tablet, opening the file of photographs. "I have pictures of my mother and me over the years, if you'd care to take a look."

For this, Malcolm did lean forward. He swiped through more than fifty pictures, studying each one for many long moments. Finally, he closed the file, pushing the tablet sharply away. "You can take that back."

She slid the device back into her bag, chilled. "So where do we go from here?"

Malcolm wrapped his arms over his chest. "That depends entirely upon you."

"Me?" She shook her head, confused. "Not at all, Mr. Maddox. I've made my move. It's your turn, to either respond to it or not. As you prefer."

Once again, that cool stare, like he was waiting for something more from her.

Something that he thought he was owed.

Which seemed backward. She'd given him everything she had to offer. She'd displayed her most intimate memories, for God's sake. Showing him that file was like pulling a piece of her heart out of her chest and handing it over to a stranger. Not knowing if it would be flung back into her face or not.

Malcolm made an impatient huffing sound. "Come on now, Ms. Valente. Is there anything else important that you need to tell us today?"

She was confused. "Excuse me? Does this issue not seem important enough to warrant a private meeting with you?"

"Skip the snark, please. Do you have anything else to say, beyond your genetic revelation?"

Sophie studied each of the people in the room in turn. She had the uncomfortable feeling that some inexplicable trap was about to spring shut on her.

She shook her head. "Nothing," she said. "This was the sum total of my agenda for today."

"Oh, enough of your bullshit." Malcolm slapped his hand down on the desk, making everything on it rattle.

Sophie jerked back, startled. "What on earth? What bullshit?"

"Come on, girl! For your mother's sake, and for everything that I should have done for you while you were growing up, I'll give you a pass. But you've got to come clean!"

"Come clean about what? A pass on what? Explain yourself, for God's sake!"

Malcolm shook his head. "Don't play dumb with me. I'll go easy on you, on the condition that you cooperate completely with our internal investigative team, and then swear never to contact me or my family ever again. But for that, you have to confess."

"But…what are you suggesting that I—"

"God knows, I'd want to get back at me, too, if I were you," he said.

"Get back at you? Hold on." Sophie sucked in a shocked breath. "Oh, my God. You think I'm the one who's been selling Maddox Hill proprietary IP to China?"

"Oh, so you know about that!" Malcolm's voice rang out in challenge.

"Of course I know! I found out right after I got here. But I didn't know who I could trust here, so my plan was to unearth the thief myself and serve you his head on a plate before I even told you we were related. But it turned out to be a slower business than I anticipated."

Tim shook his head in disbelief. "Can you believe this?" he said. "She's still playing the innocent. She waltzes in here, gets a job on false pretenses—"

"I never misrepresented myself!" she said sharply. "I gave one hundred percent to my work here!"

Tim snorted. "A little more than a hundred percent, from what I can tell."

"Shut up, Bryce," Vann said. "You don't know what you're talking about."

Malcolm turned his fulminating glare on Vann.

"You shut up. You've mishandled this from the start. You took advantage of not just my trust but also hers, which was truly despicable, whether she deserved it or not. It was very badly done, and I'm disgusted. Clear out your desk. Right now. I don't want to see your face around here any longer."

With those words, the bottom fell out of Sophie's whole world.

She turned to stare at Vann, horrified.

"You knew," she said, her voice hollow. "Even before San Francisco. You knew they thought I was the thief. You were setting a trap the whole time."

"No!" he said swiftly. "I was defending you! I never for one second believed that you could—"

"Do not hammer away at this false narrative, either one of you," Malcolm said. "We're not stupid, Ms. Valente. We have you red-handed. Video footage of you sneaking into my room at Paradise Point, taking photos of documents from my laptop."

"I was never in your room!" Sophie said curtly. "I was sent to your suite by a woman who claimed to be on the hotel staff. I was standing outside that door, knocking and yelling for you like an idiot, but I never went inside. Why would I?"

"Please." Malcolm put his hand to his head as if it hurt him. "Please, Sophie. We saw you on the video. Inside my room. Sitting at my computer. Please, just stop this."

"You may have seen something, Mr. Maddox, but you did not see me, because I was never…freaking… *there*!" Her voice rose in pitch and volume no matter how hard she tried to control it. "As if I would need to break into your hotel room to steal from you. Hah!

I could reach into your system and pull out all your deepest, darkest secrets in no time, from anywhere in the world, without leaving a trail. But I didn't, because I'm not a thief, or a spy! I have no reason to be one!" She rounded on Malcolm. "You really think this is about money?"

"In my experience, it usually is," Malcolm said. "And it looks like you got your pound of flesh, so keep it. Just take it, with my apologies. My blessing, even. Consider it your inheritance, your back child support, your payoff, however you want to label it, as long as you never show your face around here again. Do not come anywhere near me and my family. If you do, I will come after you with the full force of the law."

Sophie had to take a moment to control her expression. Tears welled up in her eyes. Anger, hurt, confusion rampaged through her. There were too many things that were breaking her heart and outraging her pride right now. She was overloaded.

She slung her purse over her shoulder and straightened up. "I'm not your thief," she said. "But I doubt anyone here has the brains to figure that out. I hope that bastard bleeds you dry. It's what you deserve."

"Goodbye, Ms. Valente," Malcolm said. "We're done here."

She turned, tear-blinded, and marched in the general direction of the door. Zack opened it for her. She was grateful not to be forced to fumble and grope for the handle. Once outside, she dug in her purse for tissues.

Sylvia called after her. "Ms. Valente? Are you all right?"

She waved her hand, shaking her head as she hurried away. No point in saying anything to the other woman. Sylvia would know soon enough. Everyone would know.

Her reputation would be trashed in this firm in a matter of minutes. And the news would spread like wildfire. She would never work in her chosen field again.

But that was something to mourn at another moment. One damn thing at a time.

"Sophie." It was Vann's voice behind her. He put his hand on her shoulder.

She didn't think or reason, just spun around and slapped him in the face with all the force in her arm.

He didn't block her, or even flinch. "Sophie, please listen—"

"You lying scumbag!" she hissed.

He reached out to her. "I swear to God, I never—"

"Do not touch me! You *bastard*!"

Their audience was growing by the second. All chatter subsided. Heads popped up to peep over cubicles.

"I never believed it was you," Vann insisted. "Never for a second, and I still don't. From the very start."

"You set me up! Deliberately! What kind of monster would do that to somebody? Why, Vann? What have I ever done to you?"

"Sophie, I didn't do that! I never—"

"You maneuvered me into a firing squad! Knowing that they'd pinned the IP theft on me. You never warned me. Oh, yes, go tell Malcolm, you said. He'll welcome you with open arms. It'll be all flowers and rainbows. You set me up to get emotionally destroyed. Deliberately. That's a special kind of evil."

"I swear, I never—"

"You thought I was a liar and a thief, but you seduced me, anyway, because you could. So why not just squeeze the situation for everything you could get out of it, right?"

"No! I never thought you were a—"

"If you'd trusted me, you would have warned me!" she yelled.

"I didn't know Tim had that video, or that he was going to show it to Malcolm before he saw you. We were supposed to meet about that tomorrow, and I was going to explain that you couldn't possibly be—"

"Stop!" She backed away from him. "Just stop. I don't want to hear it. If your master plan was to inflict maximum pain and humiliation on me, then congratulations, it was executed perfectly. Quickly, too. What did that take, ten minutes? You couldn't have done any more concentrated personal harm unless you'd hired a hit man and had me shot. Next time, maybe. Practice makes perfect, right?"

"Sophie, please," he begged. "You have to listen to me."

"No, Vann." She backed away. "I don't have to do a damn thing for you."

"Please," he said roughly. "I believe in you. I'll do anything on earth to help untangle this for you. If you would just tell me what in God's name you were doing in Malcolm's hotel room at Paradise Point. I'm not saying you're a thief. I just need to understand why you were there, so I can organize your defense. I'm on your side, I swear. Just please. Make me understand. Spell it out for me. Why were you in there?"

Sophie backed away, wiping her stinging eyes. "I wasn't," she whispered. "I was never there."

His face contracted. "Oh, God. Sophie. Please. Help me out here."

She shook her head. "Burn in hell," she whispered as she turned and fled.

Nineteen

Vann stared after Sophie. Her gleaming hair swung as she walked. The no-nonsense click of her heels faded away as she turned the corner and was lost to his sight.

People began to murmur and stir as they realized the show was over. Those nearest him, who had been frozen in fear, began sidling discreetly away.

He had to get to his office. Tell his personal staff. Make them understand what had happened. Not that he understood it himself.

He couldn't seem to move. It was as if moving would propel him into this new, awful future where Sophie had lied, cheated, stolen. Connived to cheat his employer. Used him to cover her misdeeds. A future where Sophie had been banished and disgraced, and he'd been part of it. Participating in it.

Moving, taking any kind of step…it would make this awful future real somehow.

So would standing still. Time ground forward with or without his participation.

It wasn't true. His gut, his instincts, his heart, they all refused this new data utterly.

Vann lurched forward. Left foot, right foot. The truth didn't care if he accepted it or not. He moved down the corridor toward his office. Belinda was already on her phone, eyes wide and horrified. She'd heard.

She laid her phone down. "Oh, Vann." Her voice was thin. "I'm so sorry."

"Me, too," he said dully.

"This is just…it's insane."

"I'll tell Zack and Drew to look out for your job," he said. "They'd be stupid to lose you."

Belinda sank down into her chair and burst into tears. "I don't understand it! How can he fire you? You're the best thing that ever happened to this place. Just because some thieving little slut decided to use you for her—"

"She's not a thief, or a slut," he said sharply. "She's innocent."

Belinda clapped a tissue to her reddened nose and gave him a look that was hard to misunderstand, even with her eyes overflowing with tears. It was pity.

He turned away without a word and went into his office.

He took in the floor-to-ceiling window, the deluxe furniture, the fancy decorating. This office signaled that he'd moved up the ladder in life. That he'd achieved something.

It was all gone now. The office, the job, his whole life. Up in flames, along with his love for Sophie. Everything was burning in hell, just like she'd invited him to do.

The dissonance paralyzed him, the gap between the Sophie he knew and the conniving creature that Tim had painted her to be. And Tim had somehow painted Vann to be just as bad. A lying user, out for what he could get. Capable of getting a woman's trust, using her sexually and then stabbing her through the heart.

The videos literally hurt his head, as if someone had wrung out his brain like a wet towel. What was up with that? How could it be?

The thought of watching them again made his stomach heave, but he turned grimly to his computer. Following his dad's stern training. Run straight toward pain. Like he had at high school football practice. Like when he'd been out on patrol in Fallujah.

Same thing now. He had to run straight toward the pain and the fear. Not away.

He opened his email program. The last highlighted, unopened email in his list, the one from Bryce, had two video attachments. His jaw ached from being clenched so hard.

He played the first one.

It was Sophie on the walkway outside Malcolm's room, her luxuriant hair tossed back by the wind. He fast-forwarded all the way through the hotly disputed four minute and twenty-five second window when she was in the room, and then watched Sophie come back the other way. Her hair was now tossed forward over her face by the wind. She brushed it back and took off, moving as fast as heels like hers would permit. Definitely Sophie.

Then Vann set the other clip to Play. He watched the dark, shadowy figure come into the room, sit down and wake the computer up.

In this video, she seemed different. It was Sophie's face, yes, but her expression was out of sync with the video he'd seen of her outside. Outside, she had looked worried, agitated, angry. In this video, she looked calm and unhurried. It was the look of a person in the blissful zone of pure concentration. Not looking at her watch, no shifty eyes or nervous gestures, no lip-biting or shoving her hair from her forehead. No hint of urgency or stress. Or guilt.

Of course she wouldn't be looking at her watch. There was a clock on the computer screen. But her hair? It didn't look wind-tousled at all. It was smoothed over her shoulders in perfect, freshly styled ringlets arranged decorously over her shoulders. He'd just seen her finger-comb them back off her face moments before.

This was all wrong. The look on her face. The calmness, the unhurried air. Her hair, unruffled by wind or fingers, curling over her chest.

Which was on full display. Luscious cleavage popped up over the neckline of the crinkly edge of the chiffon bodice. The fabric encased her breasts like flower petals.

He didn't remember admiring Sophie's cleavage during the party. It was the type of sexy detail that would burn itself permanently into the long-term memory of any straight man with a pulse. But it hadn't registered on his.

His hand shook as he guided the mouse to click back on the previous video of Sophie outside the room.

No cleavage here. Because the floppy pink chiffon rosette was positioned right at the level of her breasts. Not below.

He observed the indoor clip again. In this image, the rosette was much lower. Hooked loosely closed at waist level, leaving her chest uncovered.

It wasn't adding up.

But something told him that drawing Malcolm's attention to Sophie's luscious cleavage was not going to earn him any points. He'd just look like the balls-for-brains idiot that he was, wildly in love with the woman that he'd just stabbed through the heart. That wasn't going help her cause, if he—

Wait.

Stabbed. Through the heart.

Oh, God. Sophie's *heart*.

His own heart started thudding so loudly he had to bend over for a moment. The searing flash of emotion almost wiped him out for a second. Then he was out the door. Belinda leaped to her feet as he raced past.

"Vann!" she called. "What is it? Did anything happen? Can I help?"

He turned, still moving. "Yes! Tell them all that it's not Sophie. Tell everyone. It's not her, and I know it for a goddamn fact. I have hard proof!"

"Um… Vann, slow down! I'm not sure it's a good idea to rush back into—"

"I have proof," he repeated. "The video they're using was a fake. And I know who did it, too. He framed her, and he defamed her. And now he is going down."

Belinda hurried after him, panting. "But…but where are you going?"

"To beat that lying bastard to a pulp," Vann said.

Rage bore him along like jet fuel, all the way back to Malcolm's office. He heard Sylvia's squeak of protest behind him as he burst through the door.

Malcolm's face darkened. "What are you doing back here? I already dismissed you! Get gone!"

"Not until I'm done," Vann said. "I have something to say to all of you."

Zack stepped in front of Malcolm. "Calm down, Vann," he said.

"Sophie is not your thief," Vann announced.

Malcolm grunted. "For God's sake, stop letting your little head do your thinking for you. She's been exposed. Lying won't help her now. Don't embarrass yourself."

"I don't have to lie," Vann said. "I'm in love with her, yes. I'm crazy about her, and I'm not embarrassed to admit it. But it's not necessary to lie for her. The woman in the video taken inside your hotel room is not Sophie. The outdoor images are genuine, and they dovetail with Sophie's account of what happened on the day of the wedding. She was set up. This whole operation was carefully planned. But the woman at the computer? Not Sophie."

"Vann." Malcolm's voice was pained. "Don't insult my intelligence. I saw her with my own eyes. It's very clearly Sophie Valente."

"You saw a doctored video," Vann said.

"Vann, please," Bryce scoffed. "Don't do this. You saw her come to the ceremony twelve minutes after it started. You saw the videos. She has no alibi, because we were all at the wedding. It's a slam dunk. I'm sad, too, but it's time to accept it and move on."

Vann lunged before Bryce had finished talking.

Crack. His fist connected with Bryce's jaw. The other man careened backward, arms flailing as he hit Malcolm's antique Persian rug with a heavy thud.

Malcolm stared in shock. "Vann!" he barked. "How dare you?"

Zack grabbed him from behind before he could do any more damage. "Easy now," his friend muttered into his ear. "Stop it right now. Not the place or time."

Vann went still, breathing hard. He jerked his chin in Bryce's direction. "It was him, Malcolm," Vann said. "Bryce doctored the video. It's a deepfake."

"That's a lie!" Bryce blustered, dabbing at the blood from his split lip. He cowered back as Vann jerked toward him, but Vann was still restrained by Zack's hard grip.

"Keep that thug away from me!" Bryce said, his voice high and shaky. "He's gone nuts!"

"It's not a lie," Vann said. "The woman in that video was dressed like Sophie, and she'd styled her hair like Sophie's, but she is not Sophie."

"Don't try to confuse me, boy," Malcolm said. "What the hell are you saying?"

"It's a video of another woman, with old footage of Sophie's face incorporated into it," Vann said. "It's called deepfake technology. It's done with artificial intelligence. It's hard to spot. But that's what happened here."

"You're grasping at straws, Vann," Malcolm told him. "Why should you conclude that the woman in the video is not Sophie? She's in the same clothes."

"The woman in the video has no scar," Vann said.

Malcolm's eyes narrowed. "Excuse me?"

"Sophie had open-heart surgery when she was a toddler," Vann said. "She has an eight-inch surgical star over her sternum. That's why you've never seen her wear anything low-cut. If you look at the outdoor video, you can see that the fabric rose is holding the wrap closed right at the level of her chest. But whoever played Sophie's body double in the video had her wrap closed at the waist. And there's no scar to be seen. It's not Sophie. It's not even necessary to investigate the video itself, but if you did slow it down, you'd find the splices. It's a fake." He glared at Bryce. "His son, the one who was looking for Sophie before the wedding. Isn't he a CGI expert? He doctored that video. Bryce is your thief, Malcolm. Not Sophie."

Malcolm leaned heavily on his cane, looking appalled. "My God," he said, his voice hollow. "Tim. Is this true?"

Tim's face tightened, and it took him a long time to answer. "I… I'm sorry."

Malcolm shoulders slumped. He sank down into the chair. "Oh, Tim. What in God's name have you done?"

"I'm sorry," Tim repeated brokenly. "I had no choice. It was Richie. He got into drugs down there in LA. He got into trouble with his dealers. He owed them money. Mobster types. A whole lot of money. They were going to hurt him."

"And instead of coming to me and asking for my help, after twenty-five years of working together, you decide to steal from me," Malcolm said. "And to set up an innocent woman to take the fall. For the love of God, Tim. How could you do that to her?"

"You sleazebag liar," Vann said. "Sophie could have gone to prison for years."

"I had to keep them from going after Richie." Bryce pushed himself up onto his elbow. "Try to understand, Malcolm. Those men who were after him—"

"Get back down on the floor," Vann snarled. "If you get up, I'll hit you again."

Bryce looked up at Zack, who deliberately lifted his arms, freeing Vann. "I won't stop him," Zack said coldly. "You're on your own, Bryce."

Bryce's face crumpled, and he collapsed back onto the carpet. "I was afraid they would kill Richie," he said thickly. "I knew it was wrong, and of course I was sorry to do that to her, but imagine yourself in my place. Would you rather see some random woman spending a few years in a medium-security prison for a white-collar crime, or see your son tortured or murdered?"

Vann's fists shook. He looked over at Zack. "Please, get this piece of garbage out of my sight. For his own safety."

Zack nodded. "On your feet, Tim," he said. "Let's go get this thing started."

Tim struggled upright, swaying on his feet. Vann and Malcolm watched Zack lead the shambling, slump-shouldered man out of Malcolm's office.

The door fell shut behind him. The two men gazed at each other.

"So, then," Vann said flatly. "That's settled. I'll be on my way."

"I take it you're going to follow her?" Malcolm asked.

"Of course I am," Vann said. "Not that it's your

business. She's already told me to burn in hell. She thinks I set her up for this horror show. I have you to thank for that."

"Me? Hah!" Malcolm snorted. "I didn't do a damn thing! You were the one who misbehaved and got caught with your hand in the cookie jar, so watch your mouth!"

"I don't see why I should," Vann replied. "You fired my ass, Malcolm. There's no reason for me to watch my mouth with you any longer."

"Don't be such a drama queen," Malcolm scoffed. "I was overwrought. Things are not what they seemed a short while ago. You may now consider yourself officially unfired. For now at least. If you behave."

Vann shook his head. "I'm not in the mood to behave, or to be unfired. I have more important things to do right now than work for you, and I don't know how long they're going to take. Go ahead and hire someone to replace me. Screw this job."

"Don't be a fool, Vann," Malcolm blustered.

"I love that woman, you know that?" Vann said forcefully. "I want her to be my wife. The mother of my children. Till death do us part. You and Bryce killed that."

"Well, guess what, boy? You're not the only one who lost something today," Malcolm said. "Sophie came to me in good faith, and I attacked her, brutally. I destroyed my chance to makes things right with her. Vicky's girl. My own flesh and blood."

"I sure do hope that you're not asking me to feel sorry for you," Vann said. "Because you caught me on a bad day for that."

"Oh, shut up," Malcolm snapped. "Take your smart

ass and your superior attitude and get out of my face. Go get her. And good luck with it."

Vann headed for the door.

"Vann!" Malcolm called as he pulled it open. "When you find her, please tell her that I hope she'll give me another chance."

Vann turned to look at the older man. "Hunt her down and tell her yourself if you give a damn," he said. "It'll mean more to her if you do. I'm not your errand boy."

"Out!" Malcolm roared. "I've had enough of your lip! Get gone!"

Vann did exactly that, his pace quickening with every step he took. By the time he reached the parking lot, he was running as if his life depended on it.

Twenty

Sophie jerked out of the nightmare, a scream caught in her throat.

God. Every time she drifted off, she had the same ugly dream. She was naked in a cage and people filed by, peering through the bars like she was an animal on display. She huddled, hiding her nakedness under her tangled, matted hair.

Then she saw Vann, standing beyond the crowd. Their eyes met. He shook his head slowly, then turned his back and walked away.

Every time, she leaped up and rattled the bars, screaming his name. But Vann never turned around. He didn't seem to hear her.

Her own scream woke her every time, and she was freshly furious at herself for being so vulnerable, even in a dream. He wasn't worth her tears, damn it.

She swung her legs over the lounge chair and sat up. She'd fallen asleep reading an article on becoming a security consultant while lying under a canopy of drooping wisteria blossoms, and the afternoon light sifted through them, bathing her in a luminous lavender-tinted glow. Every puff of the scented breeze showered her with flower petals. A fountain gurgled in the courtyard.

She got up, stretched and climbed up to the terrace that overlooked the sea. The breeze blew her hair back and fluttered her crumpled linen dress. The ancient villa was built right on the edge of a sea cliff that overlooked the colorful, gorgeous scenic town of Positano, which clung to the side of the stunning Amalfi Coast. The sea was an endless, aching blue. Puffy clouds floated in the afternoon sky. Behind her, the courtyard was a mass of lemon and orange trees, their tender, pale new leaves fluttering in the breeze.

It should be easier to breathe here. Her happiest memories were in this place. But she'd had fantasies of showing this place to Vann. A lovers' paradise.

That was uniquely depressing right now.

To think that she'd come to Positano to cheer herself up. The Palazzo Valente in Florence was magnificent and beautiful, but too grand in scale for a single woman to rattle around in. It was made for a dynasty. She should probably sell it to some big sprawling family. Being alone in it felt like a personal failure.

But one thing at a time. There was so much to stress about. Her broken heart, her hurt pride, her damaged dignity, her trashed career, her crushed hopes. Whether anyone on earth would ever want to hire her again. She could take her pick of disasters.

But right now, her main challenge was just remembering how to breathe.

She hadn't known how attached to the family fantasy she'd actually become. Initially she'd done it for Mom, of course. Asking Sophie to approach Malcolm had been Mom's final attempt to heal that ancient wound. Sophie respected that, and had wanted to honor it.

But it had backfired in such a spectacular way. She'd been publicly rejected, in every way. By her father, her lover, even her workplace. Humiliated, disgraced, banished.

It had been too much to hope for. The family she'd hoped to join. The man she'd hoped to marry. She'd fallen like overripe fruit for the happy daydream of Sophie and Vann, blissful together. Sprinkle on some more fantasy ingredients: Malcolm welcoming her, wanting to know her. Cousins Drew and Ava drawing her into their inner circle. The noise and laughter of a big extended family. Love and sex and babies. Life's adventures and milestones, all faced together with a partner. Growing old together, hand in hand.

Right. She'd abandoned Rule Number One. She'd known it back in her smarter days, but love had made her willfully forget it. The more attractive the man, the more fatal the flaw. And setting her up to get destroyed by Malcolm—hell, damn.

A flaw just couldn't get more fatal than that.

She'd blocked all her Maddox Hill contacts on social media, and changed her phone number. This increased her isolation, but seeing online gossip about her professional reputation was more than she could bear right now.

Staring at the beautiful sunsets over the sea just

reminded her of Mom, on the terrace every evening, pining for Malcolm. Letting all of her other chances at love and marriage pass her by, one after the other.

And here she was, Vicky Valente's luckless daughter, staring dolefully at the sunset all alone. History was repeating itself.

But no. Screw those bastards. She wouldn't give into it. They could sit on it and spin. The whole stupid pack of them. Fate, destiny and all the rest.

She was changing this story, and she'd start by taking better care of herself. Buying some decent food, cooking it with care. Treating herself more tenderly. She'd give a damn about Sophie Valente, even if no one else did.

She collected her canvas shopping bags, slipped on her sneakers and headed out to pick up some basic ingredients for quick, tasty, extremely easy meals. Three stops would do the job—the fruit and veggie place, the deli for cheese, cured meats and a bottle of wine, and the butcher's shop. Operation Self Care had begun.

Usually when she was in Italy, she loved the intimacy of shopping in places where she was recognized by all the shopkeepers. Today, it was salt in the wound. Three different worried old ladies fussed over her and tried to tempt her with samples of this or that. Signora Ippolita, the butcher's wife, even insisted on wrapping up a thick Florentine steak for her, despite her protests that it was too much for a single person to eat.

She stopped for a moment outside, to rearrange the contents of her bags. When she looked up, she saw Vann across the road.

She dropped the bags. The wine bottle clanked on the cobblestones, and began rolling noisily downhill.

Vann was still there. He was not a dream, or an apparition.

Vann intercepted the wine bottle before it could roll any farther. He picked it up and brushed it off as he walked toward her. "Sophie," he said quietly.

"What are you doing here?" she demanded. "How did you find me?"

"I had to see you," he said. "I've been looking for you for weeks."

"*Ehi!* Onofrio!" Ippolita poked her head out the door and bawled for her husband. "Get out here! There's a man bothering Signorina Sofia!"

"Che cosa?" Onofrio, a tall, burly guy with a blood-smeared apron stretched over his large belly, stepped out onto the street, holding a huge meat cleaver in his hand. "Signorina Sofia, *va tutto bene*? Is this idiot bothering you?"

Sophie gave the older couple a reassuring smile. "Don't worry," she soothed. "He isn't a problem for me."

"I could chase him away," Onofrio offered. "Put the fear of God into him."

"Or chop a few parts off," Ippolita offered. "If he's the one who made you look so sad."

"I'm fine," she assured. "It won't be necessary to chop anything off." She held out her hand for the wine bottle. "I'll take that back now."

Vann gave it to her. She tucked it into a shopping bag and picked them up.

"Can I carry those for you?" he asked.

"No, thank you." She turned back to wave at the butcher and his wife.

"Everything's fine," she reassured them with another smile. "Really. *Buona sera.*"

He fell into step beside her as she walked up into the big wooden door that opened into the villa. She glanced back, and noticed that Onofrio and Ippolita were still standing on the street outside their shop, watching her anxiously. Three or four other people in the square had also taken notice.

She cursed under her breath, held out the bags. "Hold these while I get my keys."

He silently did so. When the door swung open, she gestured impatiently for him to enter.

She pulled the door shut behind them.

"Thanks for letting me come in," Vann said. "I think the butcher wanted to hack me into stewing chunks."

"You're only in here because I don't want an audience," Sophie said. "It's not for your sake, that's for sure."

She led the way through the shadowy stone arch and out into the center courtyard. Vann followed, and set the grocery bags down on the pavement next to the burbling fountain.

It was unfair, how good Vann looked in those slouchy tan cargo pants and a crumpled white linen shirt that set off his tan. His dark eyes were full of emotion that bewildered and infuriated her. After what he had done, he had no right to look at her that way.

"You're not welcome here," she told him.

"I know," he said. "Please hear me out. That's all I ask."

"I don't remember ever telling you about this place. Or giving anyone the address."

Vann's big shoulders lifted. "You told us that last

day, in Malcolm's office. That you had property in Singapore, New York City, the Catskills, Florence and Positano. That, and the name Valente, was all I needed."

"And you figured I'd come here? Good guess."

"I've been to all of your houses," he said. "Staking them out. Watching for you."

That startled her. "All? You mean, you've been flying all over the world? What about your job?"

He shook his head. "That's over," he said. "I'm between jobs right now."

"So he really did fire you," she said. "Seems like your time would be better served job hunting than chasing around after me. I'm sure you wouldn't want my criminal taint to wear off onto you. Hardened felon that I am."

"No," he said. "Malcolm knows it wasn't you."

She froze in place. Any news that good had to be a trap. Some fresh new cruelty.

"How on earth could that be?" she asked. "They were so sure."

"Your name has been cleared. I wanted you to hear it from me. I also thought you should know that Malcolm feels guilty as hell about what he said to you."

She crossed her arms over her chest. "So he should. How did all this come about?" She kept her voice cool and remote.

"It was the videos," he explained. "That girl who sent you to Malcolm's room? She was on their team. The thieves' team, I mean. Tim and Rich Bryce hired her. Bryce was selling the IP, and setting you up to take the fall. The girl you saw had to get you into position outside Malcolm's room at that exact time. Inside the room was another woman, already dressed up like you.

They deepfaked your face onto that woman's image. Rich is a special-effects guy. But I don't think it's that hard to do anymore, even for laymen."

"Ah," she said slowly. "So when I found Julie in my room that first night, she was checking out my wardrobe. I remember that she dropped her phone when I came in. She must have been taking pictures of all my stuff."

"Yes," Vann said. "After you left, I studied the videos until I finally saw it. The body double's boobs were spilling out of her dress. Her wrap closed at her waist."

"I see," Sophie said slowly, putting her hand over her heart. "So. Saved by the scar. Again."

"Yes," he said. "Malcolm was mortified."

"Good," she said crisply. "Rightly so."

In the silence, the birds twittered madly in the lemon and orange trees. Swallows swooped and darted. She had a hot lump in her throat. She coughed to clear it.

"So, Vann," she said in a formal tone. "I'm glad to know that my reputation is intact, and that I don't need to change careers. I appreciate you telling me. But it would have been cheaper and simpler for you to send a letter to my lawyer."

"I needed to see you," he said.

She shrugged. "The feeling is not mutual." She couldn't bear to look into his eyes.

"We have something between us," he persisted.

"We did have something," she corrected. "Then you ran over it with a truck."

"Please, let me finish," he said. "I never thought you were the thief. The more time I spent with you, the more convinced I was. You would never take a sleazy shortcut. You don't have weak spots and fault lines and holes inside you. You're complete. Sure of your own inner power. You know who you are and what you can do. People like that don't lie, cheat and steal. They can't be bothered."

She let out a bark of bitter laughter. "I hate to disappoint you, but I'm not exactly a poster child for inner power and self-confidence right now."

"I told Bryce that I knew it wasn't you when we got to Paradise Point," Vann went on. "But I never imagined he was framing you for theft. I just thought, if it's not you, then you're safe. I figured, let Bryce bait all the traps he wants. You'd never take the bait. So when I told you to go to Malcolm and tell him you were his daughter, I swear, I had no idea you were in danger. By the time I knew what was going on, Malcolm had already called you into his office."

She let out a shaky breath. "Did you ever believe it was me?" she asked. "When you saw that doctored video, I mean?"

He shook his head. "Never," he said. "I was confused, but I never thought you were the thief. But I hate that I didn't come to your defense fast enough. If I'd been smarter and quicker, if I'd caught the detail of the scar in time, I could have spared you all that pain. I'm so sorry, Sophie. Please forgive me."

Oh, no. Not again. The slightest little thing and down came the tears.

"Damn it, Vann," she snapped. "This isn't fair."

"No, it wasn't. None of it. You were treated so badly. And it just kills me."

"Well." She sniffed back her tears with a sharp laugh. "Please, don't die. God only knows what they'd accuse me of then."

A smile flashed across his face, but he just stood there with that look on his face. Like she was supposed to pass judgment, make some sort of declaration to him.

"I don't know what you want me to say," she said. "I accept your apology. Satisfied?"

He was silent for a long moment. "No," he said.

Tension buzzed between them. He was doing it again. Playing her, with his seductive energy. After everything, he still had the nerve. It made her furious.

"I hope that doesn't mean you're hoping to get your sexual privileges reinstated," she said. "Because you'll be very disappointed."

"I want more than that," he said.

She stared at him, her heart racing. "Um..."

"What would it take to make you trust me again?" he asked.

Sophie pressed her hand to her shaking mouth. "I have no idea. I've never been hurt this badly. It's uncharted ground."

"Then let's start the journey of exploration." He sank down onto one knee. "Sophie Valente, I love you. I want to be your man. I want to marry you, have children with you, explore the world with you, grow old with you. You're the most beautiful, fascinating, desirable woman I have ever known. You excite me on every level of my being. Please be my bride, and I promise, I will try to be worthy of your trust until the day I die."

Her mouth was a helpless O of shock.

"Wait," he said, digging into his pocket. "Damn. Important detail." He pulled out a small, flat box covered with gray silk and tied with a gray silk bow. He pulled the bow loose, and opened it. "Here."

It was a stunning square-cut emerald ring, in a classic, gorgeous design, flanked by pearls and tiny diamonds, fit for a duchess or a queen.

"Oh, God, Vann," she whispered.

"I remember you saying something on the beach, about making choices, coming to conclusions," he said. "I've made my choice. I'm sure. I want you."

"But I…" Her voice trailed off. She pressed her hand over her shaking mouth.

"After I finished in New York and Singapore, I headed to Florence and staked out the Palazzo Valente for about a week," he said. "So I was walking over the Ponte Vecchio with all its jewelry shops twice a day, going to and from my *pensione*. All those jewelers on the bridge knew me by first name by the end of that week. I know it's risky, buying something so personal without getting your input, but I felt like I couldn't come here without a ring in my hand. I had to demonstrate commitment on every level. We could always get you something else if you prefer a different style or stone."

"It's…it's incredibly beautiful," she whispered. "But… I just can't…"

"Can't what? Can't trust me?" He grabbed her hand and kissed it. "Then I'll be patient. And persistent. I'll just hang around until you can. Years, if that's what it takes."

Her face crumpled.

Vann placed a tissue in her hand, but he stayed on his knees, patiently waiting. This was embarrassing. She needed so badly to be tough, and here she was, melting down.

"I'm a mass of bruises inside," she said. "I just… don't know if I can."

"I'll wait as long as it takes," he said. "My mind's made up. You're the only one for me. You're everything I could ever need or want. I'm a goner."

She laughed through her tears and tugged on his hand. "Get up, you. It makes me nervous, having you down there."

Vann rose to his feet, and without thinking, she was suddenly touching him. His arms wrapped around her, and, oh, God, it felt wonderful. A flash flood of feelings, tearing through her. It was so intense it hurt. In a good way.

After a while, she leaned against his chest, which by now was rather soggy. She felt emptied out, but not embarrassed anymore. If Vann was going to make all those fancy promises about forever, he could start proving himself by seeing her when she ugly-cried.

When the tears eased off, she felt so soft inside. Buoyant. Like she could waft up into the sky like one of those floating lanterns. Lit up, lighter than air.

She wiped her eyes again. "Got another tissue?"

Vann whipped out the pack. "As many as you need."

"Big talk, mister," she said, mopping up the mess. "I hate crying in front of people. Now you've seen me lose it, what, three times now? A record only my mom could beat."

"It's a privilege," he said solemnly. "An honor. I'll try to be worthy."

Her face crumpled again, and she covered it with the tissue. "Oh, damn."

"What? What is it?" he asked.

"Mentioning my mom," she said. "It set me off. I've

been thinking so much about how she must have felt after Malcolm left her. But she had to raise a kid alone on top of it, while feeling all of that. It must have been so hard. She had to be so strong for me."

"I'm so sorry, baby." He kissed her hand again.

She blew her nose. "That day in Malcolm's office, I thought it was like a curse, and I got caught in it somehow."

"Malcolm did, too," he said. "So did I. But we broke the spell. I've been thinking about my father these last weeks. He was so defensive he alienated his wife and kid. He died like that. Cold, hard and alone. I want better than that for myself. I'll do whatever it takes. I'll learn, I'll grow. Whatever I need to do."

"Hmph." She mopped away her tears, and looked up. "Well. That's lovely to hear. I'm glad for you. I want to grow, too. But I'm not sure I'm ready to forgive Malcolm yet."

"Never mind Malcolm," Vann said. "How about me?"

She straightened up, gazing straight into his eyes. "Swear to me," she said. "Never, ever leave me in the dark about something important. Ever again. Not to protect my feelings, or to spare me hurt, or pain, or embarrassment, or fear. Not to avoid a fight. Not for any reason. You have to promise to be brave. Swear to me. On your honor."

His eyes burned with intensity. "I swear it," he said. "I'll be brave for you. But you have to swear the same thing right back to me. We'll learn to be brave for each other."

She nodded. "I swear."

Vann pulled the ring out of the box. "So you'll wear my ring? You'll marry me?"

She tried to speak, but her voice broke. She just nodded.

He slid the ring onto her finger. It fit perfectly. He kissed her hand, his lips lingering, reverent. "My love," he whispered. "My bride. Damn, Sophie. I'm so happy right now I'm scared. I mean, out of my mind scared. Like this can't possibly be true, and I'm going to wake up."

She laughed through her tears. "Aw. Do you want me to pinch you?"

The wind gusted, and wisteria blossoms swirled around them in a pale purple cloud, fluttering gently down to kiss the pavement stones around them.

"Oh, please," Vann said. "Just stop it. A shower of flower petals? That's total overkill, and it's not helping me believe that this is not a dream."

She laughed. "You have no idea what you're in for, Vann. Wait until I get you up to the bedroom with the Juliet balconies overlooking the sea and the vaulted ceilings frescoed with naked pink cherubs and chubby shepherdesses. I will show you overkill like you never imagined. Get ready, big guy."

His grin was radiant. "Cherubs, shepherdesses, angels, rainbows, unicorns, I don't care. Bring 'em on. Have at it."

"Ah…you mean now?"

He shrugged. "Anytime, anywhere. I'm all yours. Lead the way."

"Well. In that case…" She took his hand and tugged him toward the wide marble staircase that led to the upper floors. "Follow me."

"To the ends of the earth," he told her.

"How about just my bed for now? The ends of the earth can wait."

Their time in the bedroom left them exhausted and famished, which turned Sophie's thoughts to the goodies she'd procured on her shopping trip.

Delicious tender mozzarella knots. A wedge of aged pecorino cheese. Salt-cured smoked ham. Spicy olives. Delicious crusty bread. Ripe plum tomatoes still on the vine. Freshly grilled artichokes drenched in lemon and olive oil. Cherries, those fat shiny deep red ones. A bottle of good red wine. And Signora Ippolita's thick Florentine beef steak.

By the time the wine was poured and the table laden with the rest of their meal, Vann had finished grilling the steak. It was resting on a platter, seared to perfection. Vann served them each a big, juicy pink-tinged chunk of it, and they fell to. Food had never tasted so wonderful.

They were just starting to slow down when she heard a rhythmic buzzing sound. A text message notification. Not her phone. It came from under the table.

Vann fished his phone out from the pocket of his cargo pants. "Sorry, I'll turn it off. Just let me see if—whoa, wait. It's Malcolm."

Sophie was startled. "But didn't he fire you? Why is he texting you?"

"He did fire me, but he...wait. Hold on." He read the text. "Oh, God, he's here."

"Here meaning...where?"

"In Italy," Vann said glumly. "On his way down from Rome to Positano right now. To see you."

"Me?" Her voice broke off into a squeak.

"Yes. Evidently Drew and Zack have been passing along my progress reports. I can hardly blame the old man for wanting to see you, but his timing sucks. I wanted you all to myself for a while."

Sophie wiped her mouth, her heart thudding. "What does he say?"

"Oh, he's just busting my balls." He held his phone out. "Here, read it. Be entertained."

Sophie scrolled through the long message.

Vann. Twelve hours of silence means one of two things. A) You found Sophie, she spit in your eye and you have thrown yourself off the sea cliff in despair, or B) You found Sophie, she fell prey to your slick line and you are taking advantage of the situation like the dirty dog that you are. Ava and I will soon arrive in Positano. In the case of option A, we will make arrangements for your broken body to be sent home for burial. Otherwise, you and Sophie will join us for dinner tomorrow at eight, at Buca di Bacco.

I await confirmation.

Sophie blew out a sharp breath. "Oh, my God."

"And so it begins," Vann grumbled. "Ball-breaking of monumental proportions. My own fault for losing my temper. He asked me to tell you that he hoped you'd give him a second chance, but I was so pissed I told him I wasn't his errand boy and he could tell you himself. So that's exactly what he did. Now here he is."

She couldn't help laughing at the chagrin on Vann's face. "Well, wow," she murmured. "I'm touched that he cared enough to come all this way."

"Oh, yes," Vann said. "He cares. But he used me first. Shamelessly. He bided his time and monitored my progress while I hauled ass all over the globe, the sneaky old bastard. You wanted family? You've got it now, by the truckload. You will now have the unique pleasure of Malcolm's advice, opinions and judgment about every single aspect of your life going forward. Lucky, lucky you." Then his eyes widened.

"What?" she demanded. "What's that face all about? Is something wrong?"

"It just hit me," he said, his voice hollow. "Malcolm Maddox is going to be my father-in-law. God give me strength."

"Oh, you poor thing. How will you manage, I wonder." She set down her wineglass and selected a plump, gleaming cherry. He watched, fascinated, as she slowly ate it.

"Sophie Valente, you are a dangerous woman," he said, his voice a sensual rasp.

"Probably," she said. "But if you're afraid…if you just can't face it…it's not too late to reconsider."

He shook his head. "You're wrong," he said. "It was too late from the first moment I saw you. My fate was sealed in a heartbeat."

The energy between them made her face heat up.

Vann reached for the phone without breaking eye contact. "Let's wrap this up so I can turn this thing off. So? Do you forgive Malcolm? Your call. No judgment either way from me."

Sophie pondered the question. "Tonight, I think I could forgive just about anything of just about anybody."

"Lucky Malcolm," he said. "So. I'm confirming the dinner reservation?"

"Yes."

Vann tapped the screen. Okay. Option B, duly confirmed, he typed. He thumbed the phone off, and placed it facedown on the table. "And now, I've got you all to myself until eight o'clock tomorrow evening. Malcolm can't bother us until then."

Sophie pushed her chair back, and rose to her feet, licking the cherry juice off her fingers, then slowly running her hand down the front of her dressing gown until the pressure loosened the knot of the silken tie. She spread it open, displaying herself to him.

"We should use the time well," she said. "So? Take advantage of the situation. Make me fall prey to your slick line. Lay it on me, you bad, seductive bastard."

"Oh, man," he said hoarsely, staring at her naked body. "You're so gorgeous. I still can't believe this is real."

She held out her arms. "Then get over here right now, and let me prove it to you."

* * * * *

If you liked
Vann and Sophie's story,
you won't want to miss the next installment in
the Men of Maddox Hill series
by New York Times *bestselling author*
Shannon McKenna.

Available January 2022,
exclusively from Harlequin Desire.

COMING NEXT MONTH FROM

DESIRE

#2815 TRAPPED WITH THE TEXAN

Texas Cattleman's Club: Heir Apparent • by Joanne Rock

To start her own horse rescue, Valencia Donovan needs the help of wealthy rancher Lorenzo Cortez-Williams. It's all business between them despite how handsome he is. But when they're forced to take shelter together during a tornado, there's no escaping the heat between them...

#2816 GOOD TWIN GONE COUNTRY

Dynasties: Beaumont Bay • by Jessica Lemmon

Straitlaced Hallie Banks is nothing like her superstar twin sister, Hannah. But she wants to break out of her shell. Country bad boy Gavin Sutherland is the one who can teach her how. But will one hot night turn into more than fun and games?

#2817 HOMECOMING HEARTBREAKER

Moonlight Ridge • by Joss Wood

Mack Holloway hasn't been home in years. Now he's back at his family's luxury resort to help out—and face the woman he left behind. Molly Haskell hasn't forgiven him, but they'll soon discover the line between hate and passion is very thin...

#2818 WHO'S THE BOSS NOW?

Titans of Tech • by Susannah Erwin

When tech tycoon Evan Fletcher finds Marguerite Delacroix breaking into his newly purchased winery, he doesn't turn her in—he offers her a job. As hard as they try to keep things professional, their chemistry is undeniable...until secrets about the winery change everything!

#2819 ONE MORE SECOND CHANCE

Blackwells of New York • by Nicki Night

A tropical destination wedding finds exes Carter Blackwell and maid of honor Phoenix Jones paired during the festivities. The charged tension between them soon turns romantic, but will the problems of their past get in the way of a second chance at forever?

#2820 PROMISES FROM A PLAYBOY

Switched! • by Andrea Laurence

After a plane crash on a secluded island leaves Finn Steele with amnesia, local resident Willow Bates gives him shelter. Sparks fly as they're secluded together, but will their connection be enough to weather the revelations of his wealthy playboy past?

A tropical-destination wedding finds exes Carter Blackwell and maid of honor Phoenix Jones paired during the festivities. The charged tension between them soon turns romantic, but will the problems of their past get in the way of a second chance at forever?

Read on for a sneak peek at One More Second Chance *by Nicki Night.*

"Listen." Carter broke the silence when they reached her door. "I didn't mean to upset you."

Phoenix cut him off. "Don't worry about it."

"I thought the timing was right. We were getting along and…"

"It's evident you still have an issue with timing," Phoenix snapped.

Her comment stung. Carter took a deep breath and exhaled slowly. He tried not to lose his patience with her.

"I'm sorry. I shouldn't have said that." Phoenix carefully stepped over the threshold and turned back toward Carter.

"I'm sorry, too. Hopefully we can move on. It was nice being friendly. Maybe one day we could go back to that."

Phoenix looked away. When she looked back at Carter, there was something unreadable in her eyes. Had she been more affected by his news than he realized? Their eyes locked. Carter felt himself moving closer to her.

"We just need to get through the wedding tomorrow and the next few days, and we can go back to living our normal lives.

HDEXP0721

You won't have to see me and I won't have to see you."

Phoenix's words struck something in him. He didn't like the idea of never seeing her again. The past few days had awakened something in him. Even the tense moments reminded him of what he once loved about her. He remembered his own words… *The way I love you.*

Carter kept his eyes on hers. She held his gaze. Old feelings returned, stirring his emotions. Perhaps those feelings had never left and remained dormant in his soul. His heart quickened. Desire flooded him and he wondered what Phoenix would do if he kissed her. She still hadn't looked away. Was she waiting for him to leave? Did she want to kiss him as much as he wanted to kiss her? Maybe she was having some of the same wild thoughts. Maybe old feelings were coming to the surface for her, too.

Carter stepped closer to Phoenix. She didn't move. Carter noticed the rise and fall of her chest become more intense. He stepped closer. She stayed put. He watched her throat shift as she swallowed. He smelled the sweet scent of perfume. He wondered if he could taste the salt on her skin.

Carter wasn't sure if it was love, but he felt something. It was more than lust. He missed Phoenix. The thought of her absence burned in him. In this moment he realized every woman since her had been an attempted replacement. That's why none of those relationships worked. But Phoenix would never have him. Would she?

HDEXP0721

SPECIAL EXCERPT FROM

Can wallflower Iris Daniels heal the heart of Gold Valley's most damaged cowboy?

Read on for a sneak peek at
The Heartbreaker of Echo Pass,
the brand-new Western romance by New York Times
bestselling author Maisey Yates!

Iris Daniels wondered if there was a particular art to changing your life. If so, then she wanted to find it. If so, she needed to. Because she'd about had enough of her quiet baking-and-knitting existence.

Not that she'd had enough of baking and knitting. She loved both things.

Like she loved her family.

But over the last couple of months, she had been turning over a plan to reorder her life.

It had all started when her younger sister, Rose, had tried to set her up with a man who was the human equivalent of a bowl of oatmeal.

Iris didn't like to be mean, but it was the truth.

Iris, who had never gone on a date in her life, had been swept along in her younger sister's matchmaking scheme. The only problem? Elliott hadn't liked her at all.

Elliott had liked Rose.

And Iris didn't know what bothered her more. That her sister had only been able to imagine her with a man when he was so singularly beige, or that Iris had allowed herself to get swept along with it in the first place.

PHMYEXP0721

Not only get swept along with it, but get to the point where she had convinced herself that it was a good thing. That she should perhaps make a real effort to get this guy to like her because no one else ever had.

That maybe Elliott, who liked to talk about water filtration like some people talked about sports, their children or once-in-a-lifetime vacations, was the grandest adventure she would ever go on.

That she had somehow imagined that for her, dating a man who didn't produce any sort of spark in her at all, simply because he was there, was adventure.

That she had been almost eager to take any attention she could, the idea of belonging to someone, feeling special, was so intoxicating she had ignored reality, ignored so many things, to try to spin a web of lies to make herself feel better.

That had been some kind of rock bottom. Truly terrifying.

It was one thing to let yourself get swept away in a tide of years that passed without you noticing, as things around you changed and you were there, inevitably the same.

It was quite another to be complicit in your own underwhelming life. To have willingly decided to be grateful for something she hadn't even wanted.